D1489772

Chopin's Garden

Chopin's Garden

Eleanor Lincoln Morse

Fox Print Books

Published by:
Fox Print Books
foxprintbooks@gmail.com

ISBN 0-9729587-6-2
      978-09729587-6-9

For my parents,
Margaret Brooks & Philip Weber Morse

... the song is what remains
when everything is forgotten.

Astrid Ruff

1

The plane is lifting, the moon is the color of bright rust, glowing, misshapen, nearly full. Rivers of cars and strings of lights are shining below. I'll be back in Poland tomorrow for the first time in fifty-one years.

My name is Nadia Korczak. I was born in Bieńkówka, Poland, in 1934. Ten years later, I left behind a girl who was like a stream running through the woods. Bulldozers came into the forest. Birds scattered, trees fell. The stream disappeared. You try not to fill your heart with self-pity. You do your best to forget. You hear other stories and tell yourself there's nothing so unusual about losing a country. You fall in and out of love. And all the time there's a voice saying, It does matter, I long for it. I want to see the black kites sailing on thermals. I want to smell the cows, with their udders full of milk. Everything I've built here in this foreign place is built on sand.

I won't be the same person when I come back to New York. Maybe I'll find that Poland isn't home, that New York was never my home either. I used to have a recurring dream about sitting on the floor of a walk-in closet, half buried in shoes, looking for my own. I see myself sitting on the floor, throwing shoes over my shoulder. Not this one, not that one.

Tonight, my words are flapping along the ground like chickens, and I'm chasing behind. How to make sense of things—the lives of my mother and father, the life I left there? I know two things. Under my seat are my father's ashes. I intend to let them go into the river that flows beside our old village. And I mean to try to find my half-sister, Reba, the daughter my mother abandoned.

In 1939, millions of lives broke at once. Compared with many, I count myself lucky. I lost my grandmother to pneumonia and my uncle and aunt and three cousins, but my mother and father survived. When a war ends, people add up casualties; they count cities and oil refineries and power stations destroyed, forests burnt, rivers poisoned, fields littered with mines. What you can't count is the barn that collapses on a family dog and a flock of hens, my father thrashing in his bed with bad dreams, the photograph of my great-grandmother and great-grandfather on their wedding day buried under a pile of rubble.

I guess there's a time in most lives when it makes sense to circle back. In my case, it's to understand something that ended before it should have, to understand the anger I feel. My grandmother used to say, *All of us have sinned and come short of the glory of God.*

Siedząc w fotelu, miej pas zapięty, a sign in front of me says. Fasten seat belt while seated. I'm sitting on a wooden bench in a one-room schoolhouse, holding a pencil in my fist, learning to write Polish. Piotr Żurów and I share a desk. He liked to scrub his pencil over one corner of the page until the paper grew soft. There's the blackened paper, his smudgy hands, the rocking of the desk, the sound of ripping.

I always thought my father and I would go back together. And then it was too late. I can see him sitting on the examining table in a paper johnny. He got off the table after the lung specialist in Nebraska told him there was nothing he could do for him. He staggered a little as his feet hit the floor. He shook the doctor's hand. His hair, what was left of it, was sticking on end, out to one side.

I didn't really believe what I'd heard. We got into the car, and I turned to my father. "Why don't you see a different doctor?"

He looked out the windshield as though studying eternity. "Honey, I could see twenty-five more doctors and it wouldn't make any difference. Anyway, I've already seen another doctor."

"What about an acupuncturist or a naturopath?"

"It's too late for mumbo-jumbo."

"I'm not talking mumbo-jumbo, damn it." I began to cry.

"No one lives forever, sweetheart."

I started up the car and pulled onto the road. We had ninety miles to go between Lincoln and Grand Island, and I kept having to pull onto the shoulder of the road to get hold of myself. Every time I stopped, my father's chin lifted off his chest, and he said, "Are we there?" Like a little child. It was impossible to think of him leaving the world. I could hear the sound of his water buckets as he carried them to the barn all those years ago in Poland, the songs he used to sing.

After we drove in the driveway, I helped him into the house and into bed, got him some coffee, and went outdoors. The air was still, the sun pale above a bank of clouds. Down a small hill, an abandoned house slumped into the land like an old mule. I imagined children running up and down the stairs, a dog barking on a rope, but now—just silence. As I walked, I whacked telephone poles with a limb from a tree. Whoever was responsible for this, make them listen. Let him be, dammit! Then I was out of control crying, down on my knees and elbows. My father had no interest in prolonging his life, and who could blame him? He'd probably just as soon have taken the car and driven it off the edge of a cliff.

When I got back, he was still in bed. I brought him a dish of yogurt mixed with bananas. He gestured to the chair by his bed. His breathing was ragged, his eyes sunken.

"You okay?" I asked.

"Yeah."

"You want to talk or be quiet?"

"Sit," he said. "Talk to me."

I pulled up a chair.

"I'll miss you."

He reached for my hand. "I've had my life."

"You're not scared?"

"No." His hair was all over the pillow. I stood up and combed it for him, and he reached up and touched the side of my hand. I caught his little finger and squeezed hard, then let it go. I turned and walked over to the bureau. I placed the comb between his car keys and wallet, moved the car keys on top of the wallet closer to the mirror. *I don't know what to do.*

My father wanted to go out to dinner that night. I went in the other room, took off my jeans, and put on a red silk dress from one of last year's concerts. The dress was an off-one-shoulder style, close fitting, zipper up the back.

I've never been able to bring myself to stand in front of a mirror longer than five minutes. If I believed I could turn back time, I might have spent more time there, but the time for moisturizing lotion was twenty years ago, when I never thought of it.

I could see my father's square Slavic face in mine. His wide mouth, his large ears. The dark brown eyes came from my mother, together with the broad shoulders and height—I'm nearly six feet tall. My face looked worn but not ruined, the concentration lines around my mouth, the vertical line between my eyes etched deep.

I took my hair down, brushed it, and twisted it into a low knot on my neck—it's biscuit-colored, thick and very long, beginning to gray. I put on charcoal eye shadow, blush, and red lipstick.

My father whistled when I came out of the bedroom. "Where'd you get *that* number?"

"Concert dress."

"It's a show stopper."

I kissed him on the forehead and helped him out to the car. It was a low-slung, refrigerator-green Oldsmobile. He drove us into town slowly, ceremoniously—the last time, it turned out, he'd drive the two of us anywhere—past the Shagway trailer truck wash, and on to the shopping center, where Mama Carina's was.

The place had dark, fake leather booths. "Now there's

a guy that could sing," my father said, sitting down next to a black-and-white photograph of Mario Lanza. On the opposite wall was a mural of a woman with a mountain behind her. Her breasts flowed out of a tight bodice; she held a cornucopia overflowing with vegetables, like the label on a tomato can. A waitress came by, and I ordered lasagna and a glass of Sangiovese. My father ordered eggplant parmesan.

"Would you like a glass of wine with that, sir?"

"Chianti…I'm not supposed to," he said. "But how can I turn down such a beautiful woman?"

"You're a terrible flirt," I said.

Small salads arrived, and my father poked at his. He felt the same way about salad as he did about lawns: why bother? "How's that damn parrot of yours doing anyway?" he asked.

"Good."

"Who's looking after him?"

"Margot."

"What's she up to these days?"

"She just started a new job at NYU."

"She married yet?"

"No."

"Too bad." It was his way of saying he worried about me, living without a man.

It annoyed me. "You know, a woman can be happy alone."

"How come a man can't?"

"Do you think that's true?"

"Absolutely." He had a sip of wine.

"You could come back to New York with me."

His hand shook as he raised his glass to his mouth and

then set it down. "That's the last thing you need."

"So, what will you do?"

"Do? I plan to sit in the waiting room until the train comes..."

At first I didn't know what he was talking about. "How long do you think you have?" I finally asked.

"I doubt I'll make it to my next birthday."

"That's four months away." I wasn't going to cry again.

"Maybe I'm wrong." He was perfectly calm. "Listen. I'd like you to give the chickens to Olly when the time comes. Would you do that for me?"

"Sure. But *Olly?*" He'd been running down Olly as long as I could remember. Asking him, didn't he know this, didn't he know that, why was he giving his chickens that crappy feed? The same way he used to do with my mother in the kitchen. Except she never talked back, only fretted and fumed and walked out into the garage, slamming the door behind her. If she'd only said, "Get lost, you old buzzard," my father would have left her in peace.

Our dinners arrived, and he leaned over his plate to smell the sauce, closing his eyes in appreciation. I always liked watching him eat. Food interested him. But that night, he pushed it around his plate.

"You're not hungry?"

"I had a late snack." It wasn't true. He hadn't eaten anything. He took a couple more bites and a swallow of wine. "There's something I need to tell you," he said. His voice was husky. I recall everything about that moment—how his hands sat together side by side on the tablecloth, the downward tilt of his chin, my own hand in mid-air, reaching for the salt.

"Your mother was married once before," he said. "She

had a daughter who might still be alive."

"You're kidding. Here?"

"In Poland. She and I met around Christmas at the home of one of my cousins in Szczytno. Your mother was already six months pregnant. We sat together on the front steps while her husband went out to look at some horses he was thinking of buying. She didn't know me from a hole in the wall, but it all spilled out, how unhappy she was.

"She was married to a Jewish guy, a salesman for a manufacturing company. He made her quit the Conservatory and move to Szczytno. He told her they were going to Paris, and she believed him. Then he was fired from his job, and that was the end of Warsaw. He never intended to take her to Paris. And he made her stop playing the cello. He said he wanted a real wife.

"When was this?"

"December of 1930."

"You were only twenty."

"We met whenever her husband was away. She had a friend who passed letters between us.

"The baby was born in the spring, and then I didn't see Lili for almost three months. When we got back in touch, I told her I wanted her to be my wife. Of course back then, divorces were unheard of. When she told her husband, he beat her and locked her in a room in the back of the house. His mother brought the baby every three hours to nurse. He came after me with two of his brothers. That's where I got this." He tapped his gold tooth. "They broke my nose and a few ribs along with it."

"Why didn't you tell me?"

"I don't know."

"Even after Mom died?"

"Does it make such a difference?"

"Of course it does."

"I have no excuse." He poked at his pasta. "Your mother bribed a servant and ran away with the child, and then that bastard caught her and beat her and locked her up again. Finally he said he'd let her go if she'd give up Reba."

He stopped to let it sink in.

"Not Reba Altschul?"

"Lili tried to get false papers for her, but they turned out no good."

"She *left* her there, for Christsakes!" I pushed my plate away.

He didn't answer for a moment. "After the war, your mother tried to get in touch with Ewa Jarowska. Your friend Stefan's mother. That was after you came here. When she didn't get an answer, Lili assumed Ewa was dead; and that meant Reba hadn't made it either.

He set his fork down. "She did her best, Nadi. Don't you understand what I'm telling you?"

"She might as well have put a pistol to her head and pulled the trigger."

The waitress came back to see if we needed anything. My father told her we were finished. We'd hardly touched our food. He paid the bill, and I took his elbow and helped him out the door and into the parking lot.

"Why don't you drive?" he said.

I opened the door for him, got into the driver's seat, and turned to him. "You weren't there, *Tatuś*. Everyone was starving. Leaving when she did killed Reba. And your mother too."

He cranked down the window on his side, and the cold air blasted in. "I'm telling you, she did the best she could."

"She saved herself, and I was lucky enough to go with her."

"Hush." He rolled the window back up.

"Do you think Mama ever thought of her?"

"Of course."

I wanted to believe him. I pictured her gasping at the kitchen sink in Grand Island, beautiful, splotchy-cheeked, laboring with asthma in the summer heat. She was often out of breath, walking upstairs, making her way down the street, as though something was sucking air from her.

When we got home, my father went to his room. I could hear him working to get himself ready for bed. The springs creaked as he got in. There was quiet for a moment, and then his breathing lengthened out, scraping like a rusty gate in the wind.

2

I sat upright in bed, as though waiting for a ghost. Things with my mother were never right after we left Poland. Never right to the day she died. I still dream of her, six years after her death. There's something that remains to be said, some stubborn silence that won't yield. At times I feel sad for her, but mostly it's anger.

What I know of my mother's past is murky. She left Nebraska at eighteen with a suitcase and a cello, the recipient of a scholarship to the music conservatory in Warsaw. Her mother wasn't an easy woman. Her father was amiable and kind, but too weak to protect her. She probably intended to start life over in Warsaw.

From before birth, I heard the sound of her cello in my ears. She once said that I loved Bach more than anything when she was carrying me, that I always stirred awake when she played his cello suites. Once in the middle of playing, she lifted her blouse and saw a great rolling motion from the inside out, and then the imprint of a tiny foot against her belly. It's odd. I never really felt she was my mother until she told me that.

She was a beautiful woman, six feet tall, shapely, with a high carriage. She had the aristocratic bearing of her mother, softened by her father's temperament. Her hair was an unusual light red; in her late sixties, a wide, regal stripe of white appeared in it. Her eyes were deep blue.

How could she have married that man and allowed him to take her from her music? If she thought they'd be going to Paris, I can see it. But she was unlucky. It sounds like he never intended for her to have a life, only to be a beauty, attached to his arm. It must have been a great bitterness to her. She never lived up to her talent. She became pregnant. She might as well have been in Nebraska. Her life was over.

I can think these things and know them to be true, but I have trouble feeling anything for her. Are daughters predisposed to stand in judgment over their mothers? I don't think so. The other day, I took the train downtown, and a mother and her daughter were sitting across from me. The girl, who was probably ten or eleven, had her head on her mother's shoulder. There was affection pouring between them like water from a pitcher. You know what my first thought was? There's something a little sick there. They're too close. But that's not really true. I envied that girl.

I've never been to therapy. I've never really subscribed to Freud. I don't think there has to be a difference between loving your mother and your father unless your father's turned you into some kind of weird sex object. But when my father told me in the restaurant about my mother being beaten, you know what I felt? I felt bad that *he'd* been beaten, not her.

What would I do if I'd been her, faced with the choice between my father and the baby? I don't know. If I'd been young and knew for certain that I couldn't have both, I'd probably have chosen my freedom.

After my mother died, I found a box in her room, labeled, "For Nadia Korczak Only." She'd written down years
of dreams in small notebooks, scrawled unsteadily in pencil, as though she was rising from sleep as she wrote. I remember one in particular, written right after the war. *I was
condemned to death by Germans, to be buried alive. They were
going to harvest my hair and teeth. I was trying to reconcile
myself to what would happen, but I was still young. I wanted
to live.*

Anyone would want that. But she lied, she pretended I
was the only one. All my life, I've lived her lie.

The night Reba and Srulek came, the trees were full of
wind. My grandmother and I were in the barn feeding the
cows. Out of the corner of my eye, I saw a movement from
behind one of the stalls. "Babka…" I froze.

Reba had one shoe. Her blouse was filthy. She had a
high forehead, dark, curly shoulder-length hair, and a wide,
full mouth. *I am Reba Altschul,* she said. *This is Srulek, my
brother.* The little boy's eyes took up most of his face. Dark,
solemn, old eyes. She told us they were Jews, that their village had been destroyed.

"I don't know you," my grandmother said.

"Lili does." That's all she said. Reba picked up Srulek
and sat down on a lump of hay.

By then, German officers had taken over part of my
grandmother's house. The barn was close to the rear of the
house; my mother came out and hid Reba and Srulek in
the silage shed late that night, down an overgrown path,
behind the barn.

Inside the shed, a trap door opened into an earthen

root cellar, maybe four by five by four feet high. My mother warned Reba never to open the door by herself, but once, after Srulek died, we found her on her hands and knees in the open shed, as though she didn't know where she was. My mother scolded her, and Reba went down under again, into that damp earth that wept with moisture.

I often came with my mother after dark, down the path, over a bank choked with nettles. I brought Reba things I thought she'd like—a hair ribbon, a silk umbrella Aunt Dot had sent from Nebraska. Useless things.

Except on the rare day when it was warm, Reba wore a sweater that came down to her knees. Her eyes were black—large, arresting, watchful, intelligent. Every night, my mother closed the trap door and blew out the lantern. Sometimes we heard crying.

Reba told us she'd lost everyone during the roundup of their village. When the Germans came, she picked up Srulek without thinking and ran. It took her more than a week to find us.

Srulek wore canvas shoes and leggings with holes in them. His pants came to his knees, thick black cotton pants with suspenders that buttoned to his waistband. The pant legs hung straight, like stovepipes. His mouth was small and his ears big. He never made a sound from that first night to the night that next spring when he died of pneumonia.

One night I woke and knelt on the bed, forehead against the glass, looking out. A half moon hung over the field. Did I dream this? Two figures walked toward the woods, hand in hand, skirting the edge of the field. Reba was one of them. It took me a moment to recognize the other as my mother.

Reba told my mother that she wanted to visit the United States some day. It seemed like a crazy thing to say. I didn't believe any of us would ever go anywhere outside Poland.

"Shhh, don't think about it," my mother said. "There are troubles enough right here." By then, she must have known she'd be leaving Reba behind.

Another dream comes to me from my mother's notebooks. *I was hurrying to get to my cello lesson, walking along the road. There was a sickening crash, and a car skidded to a stop. A baby lay in the road—everyone said it was dead. I left it, wanting to get to my lesson, and then I hesitated and went back. One of the baby's legs was lying on the pavement, and the baby was moving feebly. With my heart thumping, I picked her up, held the leg where it belonged, and headed for the hospital. But all the time, I regretted missing my music lesson.*

Who was the baby? Reba, me, both of us?

3

An older man is sitting diagonally across from me, next to a woman I assume is his wife. His head is large, his hair streaked with gray, parted to the side, not quite clean. His wife has black hair, midnight blue in this light, gathered in a tight knot at the nape of her neck. Her clothes look newly pressed; her lips, too, are tight-pressed, sexless. She looks as though she's responsible for everything in their world: making reservations, packing his suitcase, reminding him not to forget the small black book he's just pulled out of his breast pocket.

I see my mother and father sitting on the steps outdoors, huddled in their coats, talking to each other for the first time. It didn't matter that they could barely speak each other's language. Nothing mattered but their two lives hurtling toward each other.

The week before my father went to war, my mother went through his clothes, mending and strengthening buttons. In the way she held his clothes in her lap, darning, pulling the thread in and out, I could feel the love between them. There was nothing abstract about it. Even at the age of five, I knew about love from the way my mother held my father's clothes in her lap.

My father entered the Polish army in August of 1939. It was one of the last summer days. The air was heavy, the sky covered with thin cloud—so thin, you hardly knew it was cloud, except the sky was white, not blue. The big tree next to our house was turning brown. My father opened the front gate and leaned over to pat our old dog, who was blind. I remember the sharp bone on top of her head. She stood without moving, swaying slightly, just the tip of her tail moving. My father's Polish Army uniform was too small and smelled like dust. His canvas knapsack was brown. My mother took his arm as we walked down the road to where the truck was parked.

The Mikolajczyks were already there, waiting in the truck. Mrs. Mikołajczyk sat in front, her hands folded in her lap, next to their son Władysław, the only son who wouldn't go to war. There was something wrong with him. He drooled, and his head rolled from side to side. Mr. Mikołajczyk and his other three sons were in back. My father hoisted me over the tailgate, and I stood in the truck bed facing them. My father helped my mother up; everyone stood, and Władysław's wheelchair was moved to make room. They asked my mother if she'd like to sit in it. My father sat beside her with his back to the truck cab and his feet sticking out in front of him. A wind came from nowhere. Crows settled in the trees. Did the crows really come? I remember their glossy feathers, their cries.

In Chełmno, on the train platform, my father held my mother a long time, and then he picked me up. "My little sparrow," he said, "I'm going away for a little while. But I'm coming back before long. Take good care of your mother." I still recall the smell of his greatcoat, too hot in the August heat, the feel of the scratchy wool on my cheek. Later,

I'd tell myself that he'd known he wasn't coming back any time soon, or he wouldn't have worn that coat in August. We watched him make his way through the crowd. People were crying, pushing, shouting. Soon, his face appeared at a train window next to a boy with a round face. The huge pistons turned the iron wheels, slowly at first, then faster and faster. The train disappeared, and then it was just the empty track.

More than half a million Polish soldiers didn't make it back. When we were reunited with my father in Grand Island, Nebraska seven years later, I hardly recognized him. He had a limp and smelled like someone else. None of us could speak, only cry and cry. When he finally found his voice, he said, *My little cabbage, you're all grown up.*

In those early weeks after he left us, he was sent to Warsaw. The army faced staggering odds. Even though Poland had the fourth largest army in Europe, with 300,000 men, they needed to defend a border more than 1,750 miles long against a German army of two million men, who were supported by hundreds of tanks and planes. The German tanks plowed through Polish soldiers, while Luftwaffe fighter planes—with a four to one advantage over the Polish Air Squadron—bombed cities, bridges, roads, railways.

On September 10th, my father was part of a division that launched a counterattack west of Warsaw, across the Bzura River. They fought hard and managed to capture more than 1,500 German prisoners. The great hope was to hold on for September 17th, when France's treaty obligations would require the country to enter the conflict. But on that day, France did nothing, and the Soviet Union invaded from the east. At first, Poles thought the Russians had come to defend them, but they learned otherwise. In the end, tens of thousands of Polish soldiers fled for the borders to mount resistance from outside the country. Until September 28th, Warsaw held on, but finally, food, water, electricity and ammunition ran out, and they capitulated. German planes had strafed civilians, bodies lay in the street, women crept out to hack flesh from dead horses. Parks, castles, homes, lay in ruins. My father escaped to Romania in early October, and from there went to France and then to England, where he served under General Montgomery. A German officer said of the Polish army that they didn't come forward in battle with their heads down like men in a heavy rain. They attacked with their heads held high, like swimmers breasting the waves. I can believe that of my father.

Finally when he was an old man, I should have been prepared to let him go. But I whispered like a child. *It's not true. Let him live until summer. And one more fall. And until next Christmas.*

4

One afternoon during his final illness, my father asked to go for a drive in the Oldsheimer. We turned west but could just as well have turned east. It all looked pretty much the same.

"You warm enough?" I asked, adjusting the heater. It was snowing lightly.

"Sure."

"You want music?"

"Not really…"

We drove along in silence for a few miles. At a rise in the road, I pulled over. "I brought coffee and gingerbread." The snow was growing heavier. I reached into the back seat, poured two cups, unwrapped the gingerbread, and laid it on the seat between us.

"I never saw her," my father said. "Did she look anything like your mother?"

"Not as tall. She had dark hair."

"The war turned us all into monsters," he said. I thought he was talking about my mother, but I was wrong. He watched the snow come down, hard pellets that bounced against the windshield. "When I was in France, I was out one day looking for food, and I came upon a girl lying on the ground—about your age." He turned toward me. "Did I ever tell you this?"

"I don't think so."

"I thought she was asleep. And then I saw the wound in her belly. She opened her eyes, and her lips moved a little. I think she was asking for water. I ran away. When she was dead, I came back and ate the three eggs that were lying beside her. I filled my belly and walked away. Do you understand what I'm telling you?"

"She was beyond help," I said.

"It doesn't get any lower than that." The wind blew against his side window. Snow was beginning to collect. He turned the car heater up. "How well do you remember Bieńkówka?"

"Perfectly." I saw the water pump at the kitchen sink of our old house, the back porch with its cracked, weathered steps. The river going from shine to darkness, day to night, over and over. The swing hanging from a tree by the pond, a girl reaching for the sky, her brown shoes scuffed at the toes like potatoes.

"Did you know your mother and I built part of that house? It was a single story when we took it over. We lived in the barn one spring and summer. It was one of the happiest times of my life."

"It must have been hard to leave."

"Your mother wouldn't have been happy there."

"And you?"

"I wouldn't have been happy without your mother." The wind rocked the car while rags of cloud rushed overhead.

"I was thinking about Władysław," I said.

He looked puzzled for a moment.

"Władysław Mikołajczyk."

"The crippled boy? What became of him?"

"You don't want to know."

"Tell me."

"They took him away. His mother never found out…"

"Those dirty bastards."

"I wish we'd gone back together."

"I don't know why we never did. I hope you'll take what's left of me." Pellets of snow turned to large flakes, falling fast. I thought of saying I didn't want what was left of him, for godsakes, not what was left. I wanted Him. Alive. Here.

He patted my knee. "Let's go back. Unless you're hell bent on going further." I started up the windshield wipers, put the car in gear, and turned around. We passed long stretches of field. Already, the road had a couple of inches of snow cover. The car slid sideways.

"When was the last time you changed these tires?"

"I don't know. I don't drive much anymore."

We had one hill to get up, not very steep. I made it to just short of the crest and had to back down. My heart pounded. We hadn't seen another car in miles. My father couldn't walk more than a few feet.

"You could go back the other way," he said.

"They don't plow over there."

"I bet you'll make it," he said.

The car fishtailed all the way up and crawled over the crest. And then it slipped and slid all the way home. When we finally made it back, my father wanted to check on his chickens.

I pulled on a wool hat. "Want your boots?"

"Nah…just look at that dumb cluck," he said. One of his silver-laced frizzles lifted his feet high at the edge of the fence, his head pivoting this way, now that way. He scratched the snow with his feet and picked around where he'd scratched. A silkie came out of the chicken house, looking like something out of Dr. Seuss. You couldn't see his eyes, only a grayish beak and feet, covered in a mound of feathers. Back in Poland, we never saw such chickens. Chickens were just chickens.

Snow melted on my father's scalp, and I brushed it off.

"Oh, the hell with it, let me get these doors shut properly. One day I'm going to fix them so they fit—" We both knew he never would. "Yes, my darlings, it's snowing, you're getting all fluffed up, aren't you?" He threw some seed into the container, turned on the water and let the trough fill. "Tomorrow, girls and boys, you'll be surprised. Twelve inches, the radio said." He turned to me. "Should be over by the time you fly out. Then clear sailing."

I took off my hat to pull over my father's ears, and my hair fell out of its clip. Except to trim the ends, I've never cut it since the day I left Poland. It's a kind of hoarding, all the way to my waist. I could never cut it. I wouldn't know what to do with my head.

I packed my bag and poked my head in my father's room. "How about a snack? What would taste good to you?"

"I'm all set."

I turned to go.

"*Mam coś dla ciebie.*" Wait a minute. He dug around in the drawer of the bedside table. "I thought you might like this." He held out a black-and-white photograph printed on cheap paper. I took it in my hands and went over next to the window. My father was sitting in an old rowboat with a friend, waving his oar in the air. Behind the two boys was a circle in the water made by the passage of the boat. I imagined the circle as the edge of a whirlpool drawing the boat down—the boys, their families, their houses and barns, a whole country. His friend, he said, was killed in the first week of the war. The picture is on the piano now, framed, my father forever waving an oar in the air.

I made one last call to Central Nebraska Home Care and closed my suitcase. The cab came, and we held each other tight. I kissed one cheek, and the other cheek. I smoothed my father's hair on one side. "All right," he said. "You better go."

When I called him later from New York, he told me that a woman named Tricia from Central Nebraska Home Care had come to make him dinner. He liked her, but her cooking was very bad.

"But who cares? I don't really give a damn what I eat," he said. It's like he was about to board a ship. What happened this side of the ocean didn't concern him anymore. It amused him more than anything.

5

Far below are the lights from a ship. Now they've disappeared, blotted out by a cloud. How strange, this weightlessness, this being nowhere.

When I think of home, I see the piano and stacks of sheet music. Phonograph records and CDs, their sound waiting to be released—a warm, human sound in the records, a thinner, cooler sound in the CDs. And there's Eemo gabbling and shrieking. When he finishes his morning stalk of sorghum, he sidles up and down his perch and whisks his toenail-colored beak on the wood.

I love the downy black feathers above his beak, arrayed in a double whorl like a small necktie, the diamond blaze of bright yellow splashed on his forehead and the nape of his neck. Even before people figured out that birds are related to dinosaurs, he reminded me of a tyrannosaurus: his eye, amber-colored, the pupil dilating with malevolence. You can see the wildness there, imagine the viney, shrieking forest that's his natural home. Pitiless. Opinionated. My way or no way. An honest bully. No mistaking where you stand.

"What's the matter with you?" I ask him.

"Nelson," he says, drooping his head.

"Are you hungry?" I bring him into the kitchen and give him a slice of red pepper. He picks it up, examines it, and drops it on the floor. He follows me into the bedroom, flies onto my shoulder, and craps on my shirt. "Hello, Eemo, hello, hello!" he bursts forth.

My mother and I left Sweden for New York in November of 1945. The sky was muddy, the sea gray and rough. Wind whistled through the cracks around the edges of windows on the middle deck. All around us was the smell of unwashed bodies. When I lay down on my back next to my mother at night, the sea swelled under my hips, and the crown of my head pushed against the wall. With every shudder of the boat, it felt as though the waves were emptying Poland out of my head.

We had no future in front of us, only the past. The past, the past. It was everywhere. I kept lifting the trap door under the floor of the silage shed, and there would be Reba. The horror of it. Back in Poland, my mother had said it was a good hiding place, Reba was safe there.

But as a child, I knew that to be wrong.

I was eight and Reba was eleven when she came, but we were almost the same size. My mother often gave her my clothes to wear. Over time, I watched her face grow thin, her bones jut out. I thought she was going to die down there in that hole, the way Srulek did.

My worst fear now is that she starved to death. But it seems more likely she'd have tried to escape after my grandmother died. In the condition she was in, she couldn't have gone far. Assuming she was discovered, she'd have ended up on a transport. But even if a miracle happened and she made it through the war, she'd still have been in danger. Her village was destroyed. She couldn't have gone to Warsaw: less than five per cent of it remained, and she knew no one. No one anywhere. Ewa, Stefan's mother might have helped her, but who knows whether Ewa made it through?

In Polish, *tęsknota za krajem* means nostalgia. The moment I decided to return, it was all there, rushing toward me like an ocean: the red, beery faces of men working along the road, a mist clearing over a field, the humid nose of Misha, our old dog, a rosary wrapped around Mrs. Domańska's fist. As a child, I used to imagine I could hear wolves howling in the forest at night. Their yellow eyes. Circling closer. Soundless paws. It's like that, the memories. How they creep closer.

6

The drinks are coming around. I'm tempted by the wine, but it will be lousy. Vodka though. If they sold Żubrówka, I'd be drunk by Warsaw.

On a Saturday at the end of January before my father died, a wet snow covered the New York sidewalks with slush. It was early, but Zabar's was already hopping. I ordered a poppy seed bagel with lox and cream cheese and a double dark espresso. At a table in the middle of everything, a man sitting opposite struck up a conversation. He was heading to Connecticut, he said, to see his grandson play in a college basketball game. His granddaughter was with him, eating something sweet and gooey. My bagel was heaven, the salmon like butter, the coffee, rich and dark. I lingered a few minutes talking to them, bought a couple of *rugelach* and turned toward home.

My hat blew away at West 95th and was caught between the legs of a man I'd seen before. He bent over, picked it up, and handed it over. His body smelled ripe; his smile was missing several teeth.

"Where'd you get the feather?" he asked.

"My parrot." I tugged at it, wanting him to have it. "Actually, you could have the whole thing if you want. It's too big for me."

He bent over solemnly—he had almost no hair—and I put the hat on him, like he was being knighted. And then he took it off. "Look, I don't want to be taking your hat."

"No, no, I make them. I probably have a dozen at home." He put it back on. People like to say New York is an unfriendly, uncivilized city. It's not true. I'd never do something like that in Cincinnati.

The wind carried everything before it—paper bags, flyers ripped from telephone poles. People were slanted into it. A sheet of paper landed at my feet, and the face of a girl looked up from the pavement. She was maybe fifteen or sixteen, dark hair, a smudged look around heavily made up eyes. MISSING, the flyer said. I put my foot on the edge of the paper and leaned over. Her hand touched her chin, like a young woman who's showing off an engagement ring, only there was no ring. *Last seen, 11/04/94…*the page said. *Find me,* her eyes said.

I folded the sheet in four, put it in my pocket, and walked on. I felt her there next to me, a young troubled life, somewhere still in the world perhaps. For the first time since my father told me about Reba, I let myself think she might still be alive.

When I got back, I took the paper out of my pocket and smoothed it out on the piano bench. "Suck the reyo!" yelled Eemo. He grabbed the cage with his beak and swung himself sideways on the perch. He cocked his head and spread his tail feathers at me. "Bird-o, friend-o!" he yodeled. I let him out, and he flew onto the top of the piano, rolling an '*rrr*' in his throat, narrowing his eyes, crooning.

The next day, I called the Red Cross and asked about how to trace a missing person. The woman who answered the phone told me to come to the headquarters on Amsterdam and West 66th and fill out a form. I tried to practice for a couple of hours before going but couldn't concentrate. In the middle of a measure, I jumped up, put on my hat and coat and took off.

In the waiting room at the Red Cross, an old woman sat on a hard plastic chair. The receptionist handed me a form and a pen, and the woman nodded as I sat down to fill it out.

Last name of sought person: Altschul
First name of sought person: Reba
Date of Birth: 1931
Place of birth: Szczytno, Poland
Where did person reside last? Piaseczno, Poland
Information on Inquirer. Current last name: Korczak
Current first name: Nadia
Complete current address: 217 West 102nd Street, New York, NY 10025
Place last seen: Piaseczno, Poland

I looked up and found the old woman watching me. She had thinning hair, a faded red color, and blue veins at her temples. Her nose was thin, her teeth large and square; she sagged everywhere, her breasts and waist meeting in an easy embrace somewhere around her middle. The gloves in her hand were so old, it was impossible to tell if they were calfskin or yellowed cotton.

"Who are you looking for?" she asked.

"My half-sister," I said. "What about you?"

"My husband and my daughter. I come here each Tuesday. Linda Kopecky is my caseworker. She say she call if she hears. My name is Maria."

"How long have you been waiting?"

"Since 1948." She studied me a moment. "Your sister is Jew?"

"Half and half."

"And you are Jew too?"

"No."

"How is this happen?"

"There were two different fathers."

"I see." Maria was wearing a plaid coat and cotton flesh-colored stockings. I saw then that the gloves were cotton; they'd been mended at the fingertips with brown thread, crisscrossed with white and pink.

"You left your sister?" she asked.

"I was ten years old. My grandmother brought her food after my mother and I left."

"You left the grandmother too?"

"My grandmother didn't want to come."

"The grandmother got lost too?"

"She died."

On the way to Slovakia, my mother and I took refuge one night in a barn where we met an old woman who told my mother about a chapel in her village whose ceiling and walls were covered with human skulls and bones. *The Nazis?* my mother asked. *No,* said the old woman. *After the cholera, after many wars, the parish priest and a gravedigger collected them.* Bones everywhere. Bones, bones.

"I'm sorry for your loss," I said to Maria.

"Life goes on." She smiled, and her big teeth lit the room. But it was the saddest smile I'd ever seen.

"Will you be here all day?"

"They close 4:30," said Maria. "These things you will find out."

I returned to the form.

"What was her name?" she asked, moving to a nearer chair.

"Reba."

"I come from Tykocin," said Maria. "Near Białystock. In 1942, they take us away on the Sabbath."

"I'm very sorry," I said. "I'm sorry for your troubles— " I looked down at the form in my lap, folded it in half, and put it in my bag. "I think I need to finish this at home." I didn't really need to go, but I'd drown in that lake of sorrow. "Would you like my phone number?" I asked, a guilty afterthought. "In case you hear anything." I wrote it on a piece of paper and handed it to her.

That night after a rehearsal, I put Eemo to bed and poured myself a half glass of vodka. Downing it in two gulps, I picked up the phone. It rang, once, twice, three times. My father picked up on the fourth ring.

"Hey, how's the old cabbage head?" His voice sounded rough.

"Doing pretty good. How 'bout you?"

"Not bad for an old man."

"I'm coming out the day after Easter."

"I'll be here."

"How're the chickens?"

"That goddamned little son-of-a-bitch of a rooster got out again."

"Which one?"

"The silver-laced. Tricia had to run around fifteen minutes, trying to get him out of the tree."

I laughed. "Where were you?"

"Sitting in bed, wheezing like an old truck."

"You could give him away."

"What would I do for aggravation?"

"Did I call too late?"

"No, no." He began to cough. "Listen," he said finally, "I'm sending you a check. I want you to buy yourself something. Don't pay the light bill with it, do you hear? Buy something you want."

"You don't need to do that," I said.

"I want to."

"Thanks, *Tatuś*. I appreciate it."

"You okay?" he asked. "You sound tired."

"I had a long rehearsal."

"You work too hard. When you come, we'll order in, you won't have to cook a thing."

"But I *like* to cook for you."

He wiffled in his nose, a sound of exasperation. "Okay, okay, you do whatever you want."

"What did Tricia make today?"

He chuckled. "Some kind of salted beef chopped up in a white sauce over toast."

"Did you eat it?"

"Of course, I didn't want to hurt her feelings. She's got angel wings."

"What?"

"Angel wings."

"That's what I thought you said."

"So what's up with you?" he asked.

"I picked up a missing person form at the Red Cross this morning."

"You don't say."

"I don't think it'll come to anything."

"Your mother should have done that years ago." It was one of the first times I'd ever heard him criticize my mother. I waited, but that was all he said.

"How often is Tricia coming now?"

"Every morning until noon."

"You need anything?"

"Not that I can think of."

"Well, I'll see you in just over a week."

"I'm looking forward."

"You take care of yourself."

He snorted. "It's all I do all day long."

7

There's a clattering in the galley and the promise of food. It's ten o'clock. The crew has pulled the curtain shut, dividing first class from the rest of us. A teenage girl behind me is arguing with her mother.

"I never said that," she says.

"You did," her mother says.

"No, I didn't."

"Yes, you did." It's like two kids fighting. *Give it up, Mom, you've already lost.*

A man makes his way down the aisle slowly. He's wearing a leg brace, like Wendell, who lived in my building for five years.

One of Wendell's shoes had a three-inch sole attached to long, silver-colored rods that supported his leg. He'd tell me stories about his ancestors and their hempen rope factories and pine forests, about riding a white horse across a frozen lake in New Hampshire and the horse slipping and getting up and running for shore, and how his brace got bent in the fall and he had to crawl back home. He told me once about how he chipped a hole in the ice of a lake on the last day of December. Just before midnight, he tied a rope around a tree, took off his clothes, secured the other end around his waist, and swam under the ice as far as the rope would carry him. "I was under there for two years," he said.

"I wouldn't do that if you paid me a million dollars," I told him.

He shrugged, an odd little smile on his face. I never saw Wendell's apartment. In a previous life, he'd taught chemistry in a girls' boarding school. I think he must have done experiments when he lived next door. Once, a green liquid seeped under his door into the hallway. Another time, an explosion blew out a window. But I never felt unsafe living next to him. Perhaps his cheerfulness and good manners made it seem that he'd stop this side of disaster.

His family had other ideas. They had him forcibly removed and put in a home. Three men came one Saturday afternoon. They flashed a court order at him; I tried to intervene, but it was too little, too late. I can still hear Wendell screaming down two flights of stairs, his cries in the street, a car door slam. I should have pursued it, but I felt there was nothing but raw power and money on the other side, and what chance would anyone have?

After a week or two, Ichiro moved into Wendell's apartment. All afternoon, he trudged up and down the stairs. When I ran into him toward dark, he had a potted tree in his arms and a knapsack on his back. He was about to speak, but I went by without looking at him. Out on the street, I told myself there'd been something annoying about him, but the truth was that I didn't want to believe Wendell would never come home.

Over the next few weeks, Ichiro came and went, and every time I saw him, I heard Wendell's cries. One morning, we came out of our apartments at the same time, and

I looked at Ichiro, really looked at him, for the first time. He had a small pot belly. He hadn't shaved, and the salt and pepper stubble on his chin made him look less exemplary, more interesting than I'd originally thought. He had thick eyebrows over intelligent eyes and a deep vertical furrow running between his brows. He wore rimless glasses and was partially bald, dark hair clipped short on the sides and back. If you saw him on the street, you'd say he was part Japanese. I learned later he was a hundred percent. We went down the stairs together without speaking and out the front door.

Near the bottom of the outside steps was a small sculpture, one of several that had been appearing there every week or so. This was a hound dog, about six inches high, made from rusted rebar, bent and welded together, the snout pointing forward. At the end of the nose was a piece of black rubber.

"It's good, isn't it?" I said.

Ichiro didn't answer, and we started down the street.

"You heading to the subway?"

"In that direction." He pulled a black watch cap down over his ears.

"Does my playing bother you at night?"

He turned to me and smiled. "I love music. There's nothing you play I don't enjoy." He asked whether I was a professional musician.

"I am. What do you do?" I expected he might be a research biologist or a professor at some university.

"I repair antique picture frames."

"How'd you get into that?"

He walked fast, as fast as my normal pace, even though he was several inches shorter. "A friend taught me years ago.

It was pure luck. When he moved to Seattle, he left me all his customers."

"Was that you I heard on the violin last night?" I asked.

"I'm afraid so."

"You're working on Mendelssohn, right?"

"I'm surprised you recognized him."

I paused at the top of the subway steps. "Do you have the piano accompaniment? If you bring it over sometime, we can try it."

"No." He looked at me. "No, I can't do that. You're way out of my league."

"Nonsense," I said. I headed down the steps as he crossed the street. Before disappearing underground, I took one last look at his retreating back. His body looked determined, used to going places.

Since Peter left, I've steered clear of men. Every so often I've called a recorded message from a classified ad and listened at a dollar a minute: *I'm a vegetarian, father of two teenage boys. I'm looking for a woman who will put the light back in my life.* Mostly, I'm fine as I am, but I have to admit there are times—no matter how many times I tell myself I'm happier alone. There's nothing to save us from these hearts we're born with.

I've been married twice: two and a half years to Jimmy, seventeen to Peter. I can't imagine life now with either of them. I can't even remember Jimmy's face, although when we fell in love, the idea that I could lose his face was impossible. Into the middle of my life he came, shiver-spine sky-diving. A train rumbled toward Chicago with us in it, its lights lonely in the night. I was playing for his dance troupe on tour. He and I sat next to each other on a narrow berth while telephone poles rushed by in the dark. He smoothed my hair away from my face and kissed me. My legs shook. He took off my shoes and kissed my ankles. He unbuttoned my blouse, slipped it off one shoulder. He took my face in his hands and gathered me against him. My fingers felt down his back, bone by bone. I pulled his shirt buttons open and undid his belt buckle as the train beat under us.

We told each other it was for life. But one night, two and a half years later, he went out for cigarettes and never came back. I found money and a note. It was like a suicide, only he wasn't dead. *I love you*, his words said, *but I need my freedom.*

I wonder if he's still alive, still dancing. He was thin as a stork. He loved jelly doughnuts. Even now when I think of him, I see jelly doughnuts. In fact it's all that's left of him. A bit of fried dough around a pillow of sweetness. It's horrible really.

And Peter? He's partially bald with wispy black hair around the ears, thick, fierce eyebrows, and a dark complexion— handsome in a brooding, Russian way. Mixed in with a kind of winsome helplessness, there's a driving ambition in him. He wants to understand the stars. He wants to know how the universe began. Small questions don't interest him. He thinks in light years, not human years. Unbearably intense at times, he's just plain intense the rest of the time. He can't stand social injustice. I can't recall one time in all the years we were together when he ever really stopped working. Even sitting on the edge of a lake, he was at it, somewhere in his head.

I ended up with him for many reasons. I've always felt there's nothing worse than being half dead, watching TV every night from seven to eleven, falling into bed, waking up with an alarm, putting on a striped shirt and tie, going to a job you hate, coming home, watching TV. I feel nauseous just thinking about it. I see a sign on a subway, "Learn How to Drive," and I think it says, "Learn How to Live." So Peter and I had that in common. But more than that, I suppose I ended up with him because he was too busy to love anyone. It fit my needs. I didn't feel I deserved to be loved. That sounds cheesy. Like I'm going to begin to sob about it.

Of course it wasn't all his fault that it didn't work out. I suffer from something—you might call it selective compassion. I hit the wall with certain people. Like my mother, and like Peter, it turned out. When he was away, I felt genuine fondness for him. But the minute he returned, I became wary. He used me up. It was like the fire went out of our hearth early on, and I could never rekindle it.

At first, sex was good enough, but as time went on, I pushed him away, the way you push away a dog with pleading eyes. The more I pushed, the more he needed. *Get away from me*, was how I felt. *Get your needs met with someone else.*

And finally, he did.

And then, I was hurt, jealous, enraged. I don't pretend to have been logical—certainly not righteous in how I treated him. Or the other way around for that matter. I might have handled his odd affair better if he hadn't lied. Probably not, though. I'm not constituted to share a man with another woman.

Peter and I probably could have gone on like that for years, two lonely people. But this time the woman was a graduate student, and he got her pregnant. She was going to get an abortion. He didn't love her, he said. He loved me, but he wanted to keep seeing her. I said no, I couldn't live with that, and he agreed to end it. But it turned out he kept seeing her for another eight months. Then he tried to come clean with another full-blown confession. "I think I really do love her," he said.

"So you're saying you're powerless in the face of this, that you have no more control over your feelings than a horse would have…Did you ever love me, Peter?"

"Of course. I still do."

"No, I mean the way you do this woman." Erin was her name.

"Not in the same way physically," he said. "No, I'd have to say it's different."

"You're a criminal!" I cried. "You've lied to me! You've lied and lied!" I threw a plant at his head and missed. It was like an explosion, one moment the roof attached to the house, the next moment our lives blown apart. I couldn't bear to have him near me.

After he left, I found the condoms in his bedside drawer. He and I didn't use condoms. Had they made love in our bed? Kimono MicroThins. Sheer pleasure, the small packets said. 38% thinner. I opened the window and hurled them out. In the light of the street lamps, they landed on the sidewalk, in the branches of trees. I wanted to throw everything into the street, empty the rooms one by one. The sound that came from my throat was something I'd never heard before—sorrow and howling rage, the sound of an orphan.

My pride wouldn't let me feel sorry for myself. But I felt stupid. Stupid! Stupid! Like someone just off the boat, carrying a cardboard suitcase, wooden clodhopper shoes on my feet. Margot said after Peter and I broke up that she'd often wondered when I'd see the light.

I've seen two loves die now. Everything about love feels precarious to me—like life itself, lived in the shadow of its own brevity.

In America, people believe you can start again. History carries no weight. Move to San Diego. Move to Chicago. But I don't believe you ever start over. Everything that's happened keeps on going. I imagine a mastodon long ago, dying in a swamp. A molecule on her tusk was carried somewhere. And then somewhere else. Nothing ever ends.

I have no children. Do I regret it? Peter is a mathematician and black hole theorist, working at Columbia. *Imagine an object so massive,* he explained to me when I first met him, *so densely packed that not even light can escape its gravitational pull.* I used to picture a vortex in the starry heavens pulling whole galaxies into itself, star after star gliding toward the great dark gap, passing through the boundary between return and no-return, moving closer, inexorably toward oblivion. With Peter, my womb was a black hole. Children disappeared in it.

A month after he left, Peter asked me to lunch. Margot said it was a bad idea. Actually, she said a lot more than that. "Why should you succumb to his guilt-ridden, misguided, pseudo-rational crap about being friends? Why does he think you need to be friends? You'd be *with* him if you wanted to be friends. He's a baboon." But I didn't pay any attention to her.

Peter and I sat miserably in some restaurant. I couldn't eat. He ordered a chopped herring sandwich.

"Why couldn't you at least have told me?" I asked.

"I don't know."

"It's none of my business—but are you happy with her?"

"We're not together. She's with someone else."

"Oh."

"When I look at young men in my classes," he said, "I envy them. Their lives look so straightforward."

"They're fucked up too. Everyone's fucked up."

"I still love you, Nadia."

"Why would I want to know that? Don't tell me that."

"I was thinking maybe we could get back together."

Until then, I'd felt a little sorry for him. But then I didn't. "You can stick your love up your ass. Don't you know anything? Don't you see what you've done? We're finished. Don't be expecting we're ever getting together again. We're so done, Peter, I can't even tell you how done we are." I got up from the table, intending to leave, and then I felt silly and sat down and began to cry.

8

I overheard one of the Polish airline crew say their pay went down last week. They've passed out dinner and drinks; now they're in the galley kitchen, chain-smoking in a bad-tempered clump.

The man sitting on the seat beside me is ripping open the cellophane that holds the napkin and silverware. He has large hands, the color of earth. He's concentrating hard on his chicken dinner, a crease between his eyes, mouth slightly parted. He has sideburns and a heavy morning-after shadow.

I taste the rice.

He looks over and says, "My name is Rishi."

"Nadia." We shake hands.

"In my country, women are not so tall as you."

"What country is that?"

"India." The only thing that interests him is my height. It often surprises me that people see me this way—it's something that just *is*, nothing I ever think about.

"What were you doing in the U.S.?" I ask.

"Recently I was completing my Master in Divinity degree," he says. "And now I am going to visit the Black Madonna in Czestochowa and the birthplace of His Holiness,

Pope John Paul II in Wadowice, after which I will return to Bombay."

"You're a priest?"

"I have completed my education, but I have not yet been ordained." He finishes the main course and begins on a piece of angel food cake. A single red raspberry sits on top like a polka dot. He eats the berry and falls comfortably silent.

During my mother's last days, my father drove to the grocery store and brought home small boxes of raspberries. He climbed the stairs and fed them to her, one by one, like a bird passing a berry from one beak to another. My mother's eyes had the same look I'd seen in Reba's. That flat calm, where loss at its extremity goes. It falls to the bottom of the river like a pebble, where it watches the sun and shadow move over the surface of the water above it.

My mother didn't want to leave the world. Neither of us knew what to do for her. My father wandered through the house in the middle of the night and out into the chicken pen to sit on the bench, nodding off like a rooster. I made my mother sweet puddings: bread puddings, lemon puddings, custards, apple Brown Betty. She ate them all. She ate everything I gave her, as though it was her job. Only once, when I was sitting by her bed in the dark, did she talk about what was on her mind.

"I'm afraid," she said. "My life feels loose."

"What do you mean, Mom?"

"I'm looking for something."

"Something you lost?"

"Yes, that's right. Something's missing."

"Can I help you find it?"

"If you would, yes."

"In one of these drawers?"

"No, no." The light fell slanted through the window. Her hands kneaded wildly in the air. "Not there."

"Where, Mom?"

"I don't know." She started to cry. She couldn't tell me where to look. A few days later, she died.

I felt her innocence, her life scaled down, distilled to her natural beauty. I was washed in her loss, washed in my own. Her beautiful bright eyes, her cheekbones, had vanished just like that.

What to forget, what to remember? Codrescu, the Romanian, says this question is a tension peculiar to exiles. I think it's a question peculiar to anyone alive. Scenes rise like ghosts and float away: my mother's hands in the air.

What was it like for her? I know so little. She left the U.S. for Poland as a young woman. She came back to Nebraska in 1946. Her father was dead. Her mother was an electric storm, bigger than life, with a jagged beauty, irascible, unpredictable, task-driven. There was little fondness between the two of them, more of a dutiful formality.

We lived in my mother's girlhood home for nearly a year after we left Europe. My mother needed to get permission before she did anything in the kitchen; in private, she called her mother *The Duchess*. Once to her face. Most of their spats were behind closed doors, after which my mother would appear, thin-lipped, her head sitting higher than usual on her neck. After my father arrived and we moved to our own house, we saw my grandmother only every few months, even though we lived ten miles away.

9

I imagine the small lights of this plane traveling through the night, through black winds. From below, to anyone looking up, we'd be a single white light, moving slowly through the sky. Inside, the flight attendants are clearing trays. One of them, his hair in a brush cut, stuffs things in trash bags angrily, as though he was born to nobility and ended up working on this plane by accident. Rishi, the priest, has pulled a blanket up around his shoulders and gone to sleep. Across the aisle, a woman is holding a baby in her lap. The mother's eyebrows are plucked thin. She's wearing a lacy dress with her bra showing through at the back.

A few months ago, I returned to the Red Cross with the filled out form. The receptionist said the office was in contact with the International Tracing Service in Arolson, Germany. She didn't offer much hope but said you never know—people can wait for years, and then, all of a sudden, there's something.

One day, not long after, I came home and found a message waiting for me. "Nadia?" said a voice. "*Dzień dobry.* Maria here. *Chcielbyśmy zaprosić was na kolację na wtorek wieczór.*" We'd like to invite you to dinner next Thursday.

I wondered who the "we" was. I called her back and

said I couldn't do Thursday, but the following week was good, the 17th.

"Yes, that's the one I am meaning." She gave me directions.

"Can I bring something?"

"*Nie, nie.*" Nothing. I will cook. *Wieprzowina. Kapusta.* You like this?"

Brooklyn. A dark, lonely hallway in a fifties apartment building, light green walls, peeling paint. A door closing somewhere below. I knocked on the door and heard footsteps inside. Maria's face appeared, flushed with cooking. I gave her the flowers in my hand.

"*Dziękuję. Prosimy, prosimy!*" Come in, come in. She hugged me. "I forget you are so tall." The smell of cabbage filled her place, my grandmother's smell. My mother used to say, *Every woman should have her own scent.*

Jean-Paul Gaultier, Yves Saint Laurent. Cabbage.

Maria took my coat to the bedroom. The apartment was tiny, crammed with furniture. On the floor, a maroon carpet lay on top of a beige rug. On a small table was a porcelain ballerina sitting on a lace doily. Two layers of curtains hung at the window, sheer ones that filtered light, faded yellow ones over the top.

"He didn't hear you," Maria said, coming out of the bedroom with a little dog behind her. "Yes, Pootsie?" He barked and ran around and around in circles. His tail was a little plume. I reached down to pat him, and he flopped over on his back. I scratched his tummy while one of his back legs went up and down—boing, boing.

"*Siadajcie,*" said Maria. Have a seat. "*Czego się napije-*

cie?"

"*Dla mnie cokolwiek.*" I'll have whatever you're drink-ing.

When Maria was out of sight, Pootsie grabbed me around the ankle and humped my leg. I shook him off, and he began again. "Pootsie, no."

Maria returned with two glasses on a tray. "Vodka," she said. She gave me one, sat down, and raised her glass.

Pootsie began to pump again.

"He likes you," said Maria.

I drank half a glass quickly.

"Real Polish vodka," said Maria. "Special for you."

"*Znakomita.*" Excellent.

"He's naughty boy." She pointed to a corner of the rug that was gnawed in a half-circle. "Pootsie did." Maria held her hand high, a dog biscuit between two fingers. He turned around and leapt for it.

"I have a bird," I told her. "A parrot."

"What's his name?" asked Maria.

"Eemo."

"Funny name."

"He used to live with a Turkish fellow." I downed the rest of the vodka.

Maria stood up.

"Can I help with anything?"

"*Nie, dziękuję. Już wszystko gotowe.*" No thanks. She disappeared. The oven door opened and shut. A cupboard banged. Maria went in and out of the kitchen with steam-ing bowls and finally, "*Proszę do stołu.*" Please. Come to the table.

It was overwhelming. Beef brisket. *Pierogi.* Cabbage. Beets. Roast potatoes. *Kompot z jabłek.* A cold omelet cut into triangles. All laid out on a red tablecloth. "More vodka?"

Yes. I said yes to everything.

"Special for you," said Maria. "My friend Adara Spaneas live downstairs, and I teach her how to cook Polish and she teach me sometimes Greek food. Last week it was *pastitsio,* do you know it?...No?" She wrinkled her nose. "Lot of trouble for what? She don't really like Polish cooking too."

Halfway through dinner, I asked if she wanted to tell me about her husband and daughter.

She refilled our glasses and said that the men in the village had all been loaded into trucks from the synagogue, where they'd been praying. "Then they make the rest of us go to a big field. They push the big children and women over on one side, and they take the little children and babies away. I can't tell you."

I bow my head.

"On the train, my friend Ilana whispers to me. We hide between the cars, and she says, 'Now!' and we jump. They shoot at us, but I don't care if we die, it's all the same. We meet Bogusław, an old man. We don't know him, but he takes us to the place over his kitchen in the what do you call?"

"The attic?"

"Yes. He brings us food every day, every day. After the war is finished, he says they are still killing the Jews and I must leave Poland. So I come here with his help and the grace of God."

"What about Ilana?"

"She died." She patted her chest. "She can't breathe. Is too bad for her. She wants to live, and I want to die, and look what God does. What for? Maybe He think I'm good for something, but I don't know what. *Der mentsh trakht, un Got lakht.*" A man thinks, and God laughs.

Maria got up from the table with the bowl of potatoes and staggered into the door jamb. I picked up two bowls and followed her. "Don't worry," said Maria in the kitchen. I put my arm around her, and she leaned her head against my shoulder.

She opened the refrigerator. "I make a pie for you." It was impossible to eat any more, and I knew I'd eat a piece if it killed me.

"Chocolate buttercream," said Maria taking it from the refrigerator. "Do you want coffee? Yes?" She knocked the kettle to the floor, picked it up, and filled it at the sink. "But this is what happens," said Maria. "They find records of others from village, almost all died at Majdanek, but nothing saying Jacob Horowitz. So maybe he escape like me? You never know."

Pootsie came into the kitchen with a leash in his mouth. "You want out, Pootsie? All right. You want to come with us, Nadi?" Maria got our coats, and Pootsie trotted toward the stairwell. All the time she was talking—about the other people in the building, the way the landlord hadn't fixed the hot water for a month.

Clouds swept the sky. It had rained, and the night was fresh. In a street light, the first green leaves were visible. Maria took Pootsie off his leash. He scratched his back legs on the sidewalk and ran at invisible dogs, veering off into the shadows.

"What do you do?" Maria asked. "Do you work?" She'd asked me this before but seemed to have forgotten.

"I play the piano."

"People pay you when you do it?"

I laughed. "Yes."

"I was working in hospital laundry. In the summer it's so hot people fall down. They have no fans down there. But I like the people I work with. From Argentina, Mexico, Phillipines, even Poland."

"Do you miss it?"

"No, no, I don't miss. Now I am retired."

When we returned, Maria refilled my glass and cut two large pieces of pie. We sat down, and she grew quiet, almost prayerful, as I took the first bite. "Is good?"

"Delicious," I said. She talked about the *piernik* her mother had made at Christmas when she was a child. About the *rózga* attached to the bag of candies for her brothers and sisters, the biggest birch rod for her younger brother because he was bad and needed a big stick.

When it was time to say goodbye, Maria said, "God brought you to Red Cross on Tuesday. Maybe you go Wednesday, and we never meet." Her hair was damp and pulled back in a loose knot at the back of her neck. I saw her leaping from the train, her body suspended in air, her skirt pressed against her as the wind caught it. Long grass grew by the side of the tracks, breaking her fall. Her friend ran for the woods, and Maria ran blindly behind her.

I opened my arms and pressed my cheek against hers. I felt all at once that I loved her. "*Do widzenia. Bardzo mi było przyjemnie,*" I told her. I've enjoyed myself so much. I gave Pootsie a pat and closed the door behind me. After one night, Maria understood most things better than friends of twenty years: how a life gets dismantled. All you had to do was look into her face to read it all, that unmistakable ocean of loss, the tilt of her head that said, There's no bringing it back.

10

I'm waiting in line for the bathroom. A young black guy stands in front of me, and we fall into conversation. His face is dented here and there from what looks like chicken pox. His eyes are mild and alert. He's heading to Warsaw to work on a film, he says. I'm about to ask him more, but someone comes out of the bathroom, and he goes in. The black-haired woman is leaning against her husband's shoulder. Her lipstick has grown dull from dinner. Asleep, she looks like a little girl.

One day in February, Ichiro and I met on the stairs, and he invited me for a cup of coffee. I was going for a walk, but I told him I'd stop in on my way back. If I'd had an excuse, I'd have used it. I'd been thinking it was a good thing he'd refused to play duets, that it was best with neighbors to be friendly and neutral, on the formal side. If things got too chummy, you came home needing quiet, they heard you come in, and before you knew it, you were into a forty-five minute conversation. But I wasn't quick enough to come up with anything.

Outside, the air was raw, springtime light suffusing the buildings and pavement. In the park, sweet gum trees dripped with moisture. The river looked iron-gray and still in the distance, concrete and brick high rises on the far side. Dark limbs of trees were outlined against the gray water and sky, sharp boundaries everywhere, the world in black and white.

I often visited a particular beech tree down there, an old survivor. I thought of it as my father's tree. Two years earlier, half of it split off, and the tree people worked on it and shored up what remained. It was beautiful in every season, naked branches reaching for the sky in winter; in spring, green against gnarled limbs.

On the way back, I went into a bakery and bought cookies.

Up 102nd Street, the soprano was practicing, her wide vibrato spilling onto the street like fuchsia paint. And then the canary-yellow building I call home—with its by-gone, ersatz Corinthian white columns and the ovals and curlicue trim framing the door. It's a silly building really, no other word for it. When I came into the lobby, I caught a glimpse of myself in a small, brass-framed mirror hanging on the wall: a young woman inside an older woman—the same big bones, the same eyes, same wide mouth, my unruly hair tucked under a hat. But I noticed something around the eyes that hadn't been there before—some hint of mortality: *I'm on borrowed time.* I started up the stairs and tripped on the bottom step, caught myself with my hand on the rail. In my fist was the small paper bag, stained with grease.

"I brought us cookies," I said when Ichiro opened the door.

"I burned the mochi cake," he said.

"What's that?"

"A rice cake. The fire alarm just stopped." The window was wide open.

"Is it salvageable?"

He opened a metal wastebasket with his foot and pointed to a heap of charcoal. The wastebasket came down with a clang. "I was working on something and forgot the oven was on. I'll show you what I was doing." He closed the window, poured two cups of coffee and led the way out of the kitchen. Behind three *shoji* screens, taking up the whole living room, was his workshop. A picture frame lay on a table, the ornate trim broken in half.

"You can fix this?"

"It's not so hard," he said turning the frame over. "You start with the substructure. See here? The corners have separated and need bringing together. I always preserve what I can, especially the original maker's marks." He pointed to thick pencil marks.

"Then I have to stabilize the plaster cracks—here's an example. I'll show you." He put a paint brush in either of my hands. "With one hand, I brush the crack with denatured alcohol; with the other, I brush rabbit hide glue. The alcohol makes the glue permeate deeply. Then I make individual molds for the missing sections, using part of the frame pattern that's still whole. So for this broken spot here, see? I'd go across where the pattern's symmetrical and create the mold." On two walls were banks of flat wooden drawers, each drawer with a different kind of drawer pull made from odd bits of wood. He pulled a sample from a flat drawer and gave it to me.

"Once that's dry, I cast epoxy putty into it. Then when I've got the new piece, I carve it to fit into the broken area. There's a lot of shaping and carving. If there's nothing to cast a mold from, I carve a piece to fit, free hand."

Then, surprisingly, he stopped.

"I'm boring you."

"Do I look bored?"

"I don't know you well."

"No, I'm not bored, I swear it." I was speaking the truth. His words didn't really interest me, but his hands did. I think of them now as having a kind of brightness, constantly moving, like flags in the wind.

"All right, I'll just show you one more thing." He rummaged around in the drawers. "Gold leaf. This is the fun part. Usually, you apply it to a gesso ground. If the original gesso is separated from the substructure, you have to reapply it. Right here, I'll be putting on several thin layers. You have to sand between layers. Then three to four layers of bole."

"What's that?"

"You can often tell whether an old piece is from Italy or France or this country by the color of the bole—yellow, gray, or red. It's a soft, oily clay. While the final layer of bole is still wet, you lift the gold leaf and place it over the top.

"The leaf is extremely delicate to handle." He went to another drawer, took out a sample and handed me a tool. "You use it like a brush, you see? It's called a gilder's tip. Give me your hand." He gently tapped a piece of gold between my thumb and first finger and smiled. "A gilded pianist…You have nice hands," he said, blushing.

He covered his confusion by putting a tool back in one of the drawers. "…I haven't told you about finishing techniques, but that's enough."

I couldn't imagine doing this work all day and told him that.

"It's less boring than it looks. I'm my own boss, and every piece is different."

"Who do you work for?"

"Museums mostly, but private collectors too."

I took a sip from one of the cups on the table.

"Is it all right? It's cold, isn't it. Here I'll warm it."

"Don't worry."

"Let me warm it."

"No, no, I often drink it this way."

"Well at least come sit down." He led the way to a small room off the living room. He'd built a shelf along one wall and filled it with magazines and books. The rest of the room was taken up with a modest-sized Oriental rug and two upholstered chairs on either side of a table. On a side wall was a watercolor, a good one, of a road leading between poplar trees.

"Your apartment's laid out exactly like mine, but it looks so different."

"I'm a minimalist. I like rooms you can think in."

"You wouldn't be able to think in my place."

"Do you like it that way?"

"Not especially."

"I need quiet," he said. "The older I get, the worse it is. I've just started to meditate. Next step is monkhood." He smiled. "When I was a child, my father used to go to the temple. He was really more interested in the social aspects and the form—the incense, the chanting. We had an altar to the ancestors in our apartment."

"My parents weren't anything."

"No?…I have a friend who encourages me to go to the zendo. Mostly, though, I just sit on that cushion." He pointed to the corner. "I look at the wall and count to ten and watch my breath go in and out. When I'm finished counting to ten, I go back to one and start over again."

"What happens then?"

"I keep going back to one." He leaned forward in his chair. "Something happened a few weeks ago, but as soon as I noticed it, it was gone."

"A vision?"

"An illumination. Like the glow of light on the horizon."

There was a banging coming from the direction of the kitchen. "What's that?"

"The radiator."

"Mine don't do that." I finished the coffee. "I should go," I said, standing up.

"Don't go."

I laughed. "All right." I sat down again, and that was the moment our friendship began.

"Have you lived here long?" he asked.

"About thirteen years. I thought about moving to Brooklyn, but I prefer Manhattan."

"I lived in Brooklyn Heights for years. My father taught at City College. I have four younger brothers. Tokuji, Tokoji, Kenji, and Koji. They're all married, living in New York, except Koji, who's in LA."

"Are your parents still alive?"

"No." He pointed to the poplars. "This is one of my mother's watercolors."

"It's lovely. I noticed it earlier. There's a beautiful light shining out of it."

"That's what she left me with, that light."

"My mother was a musician, a cellist, from this country. My father's Polish. I came here when I was twelve."

"That must have been hard."

"After all these years of being here, I'm still a foreigner.

I feel surrounded by people who know nothing about the world I grew up in and don't particularly care. America likes to think of itself as welcoming—*Give me your tired, your hungry*—it's bullshit really. People have these bedrock assumptions, they don't even know they have them. Why is there so little curiosity about what it means to be from somewhere else? In the political sphere, the same thing's true. England and the U.S. were largely responsible for the Soviet occupation of Poland after the war. I'm not saying the U.S. didn't do its part in the war, but Poland was their ally, and FDR and Winston Churchill bargained half the country away at Tehran in 1943 and the whole of it at Yalta. Neither country really considered what it would mean to the Poles to lose a country they'd fought so hard to defend. They neglected to think of the needs of a country they considered unimportant. What happened was pure political expediency that had huge consequences for millions of people."

I looked at him and stopped. "I'm ranting," I said, "I'm sorry."

"I happen to agree with you. We don't live in a country that looks all that far beyond its borders. But I can't imagine living anywhere else—I guess that makes me provincial too. On the other hand, I still count in Japanese. That's how I first learned. You can change your language, but you don't ever change how you count…My ex-wife used to count in English out loud, but her lips moved in Japanese when she counted to herself."

"Tell me about her."

"Another time." He stood up suddenly and went in the other room. I heard him open a drawer and shut it. He reappeared with a white envelope. "Perhaps you'd like to see these." He passed me a stack of photographs, and I began turning them over.

"That was my great-grandmother and grandfather after they came to Oahu," he said.

His grandmother had thick, dark eyebrows and a no-nonsense mouth. She wore a full-length skirt that draped against her legs, and a patterned shirt. Standing next to her was a little girl in a straw hat, white dress and white stockings. Ichiro's great-grandfather looked gravely at the camera from under a bowler hat. In his arms was a baby with a crocheted hat and striped leggings.

In another one, his father stood behind his mother under a tree. His black hair was combed back off his forehead. His mother was sitting on a bench; her eyes were clear and wide-set, her mouth parted slightly. Ichiro stood behind her, a little in front of his father. His mouth, like his mother's, was parted; his hand rested on her shoulder. He was wearing a white shirt and necktie; his eyes were bright and eager. His brother, Kenji, small and serious and round-faced, leaned against Ichiro. Tokoji, the next youngest, wore a sailor suit and broad-brimmed hat and held his hands straight down at his side.

"My mother was a Christian," he said. "But she didn't push it down our throats. One by one, we stopped going to church when we were old enough to make up our minds. It must have been painful for her."

The pictures moved me. And *he* moved me with his quiet ways. I finally got up to leave when it was getting dark. "You know, I haven't forgotten the Mendelssohn," I said, standing on the threshold.

"I'd only make a fool of myself."

"Why would you say that?"

"You're a professional."

"I'm not going to argue with you." I took his hand a moment and thanked him.

Back in my apartment, Eemo was listening to a debate on the radio between a liberal and conservative. Over a drumming of antagonistic voices, Eemo gabbled wildly. I flipped off the radio and opened the door of his cage. "You're overstimulated," I said.

"Suck the reyo!" he yelled.

"Take a deep breath and let it out slowly," I said. I might as well have been talking to myself. I wished I hadn't ranted on about being foreign. It felt cheap in the face of those photographs.

But it was true what I'd said: I'm an outsider. I'm sitting in this airplane seat right now like a Polish peasant—like my grandmother sitting on a milking stool.

Above my piano at home is a poster by Stasys Eidrigevicius, a drawing of a face—it's hard to say whether it's a man, woman or child. The color of the skin is chalky, the lines simple. The eyes draw you to the face, the way they look out at the world, self-contained, nostalgic, whimsical. The sensibility—with its mixture of pity, hope, and misanthropy—is so familiar; there's no way it could have been drawn by an American.

People all over the world wash up on foreign shores. They journey along their private tracks of memory, leftovers from disappeared worlds. You can't reclaim a country. The way a sculptor chisels off a piece of stone, it's gone.

One summer evening in Memphis, I heard a calliope. A traveling theater troupe set it on the deck of a revival steamship that stopped at towns along the Mississippi. The thing started up. It made the most outrageous, bawling noise.

Like twenty thousand balloons released skyward. It felt big enough to bring down an airplane. I began to laugh. The tears rolled down my face. The sound was too huge, like a great fat person I couldn't put my arms around. A little boy said to his mother, *What's wrong with that lady, Mama?* The mother looked at me, and I heard over my own laughter, *I reckon she's drunk.*

Inside me tonight, flying over this dark ocean, Poland feels like that calliope.

11

If I were home, I'd have already put the flowered curtain on Eemo's cage. I'd be sitting in the faded green chair by the piano having a nightcap with Eemo asleep beside me.

When Peter gave me Eemo a few years back for my birthday, he led me down the hall toward the bedroom. "Close your eyes," he said. Maybe he'd unconsciously found me a new companion—it wasn't long before he made his second confession.

Eemo let out a shriek, and I said, "Stop it! Stop that horrible noise!" I fed him with pliers for a month, I was so scared of him. Music calmed him down. Bach especially. We had that in common. And gradually, he insinuated his way into my heart.

"Oh! oh!" he wailed the night before I left, with his feet hooked over the edge of the piano.

"Look what I've got for you." He was on his perch at the window, glassy-eyed, floating between two worlds. "Eemo, wake up, look in the bag."

"Mmmm," he said, not looking.

"No, look, really look." I lifted out a packet of chicken.

"Did you ever!" he chuckled. "Did you ever! Did you

ever!" he crowed, clicking his tongue and popping his cheeks.

I went into the kitchen and turned on the oven. I'd been planning to eat half and give the other half to Eemo, but I often lose my appetite when I try to eat what he eats—like being at the table with my great Aunt Lydia Bartoszewski, who dribbled wild mushroom soup down her chin, a drool of gray cream mixed with earthen dots of mushroom.

"All I want is you!" Eemo screamed in the other room.

I took off my shoes, poured a glass of wine, and went in and sat next to him. He turned his head to one side and eyed me. "Aren't you the Romeo," I said. Spring was blowing in through the cracks around the windows. The birds were back, pumping their wings over the city, landing in the park with their great wild singing. The smell of chicken poured from the kitchen. "Oh, weyy! Oh, weyy!!" Eemo yelled, parrot-weeping by the window.

Half an hour later, the short green feathers on the top of his head were covered with grease where he'd rubbed his feet through them. His cheek feathers shone as he held a thigh bone up in his right claw and inspected it. He had a savage look in his eye. He cracked the bone with a single bite, split it lengthwise, and scooped the marrow out with his tongue. His swing perch was slick with grease.

Finally, he leaned into the bars of his cage. "Ready for bed?" I asked.

He locked his legs, ground his beak, and made little clicking sounds, the way he does every night before sleep. His head was under his wing even before I got the cover on. I was walking down the hall when I heard a plop on the bottom of his cage. The greased perch.

12

The stars are extremely bright tonight. Orion with his belt and sword. The Pleiades. Cassiopeia. But the air inside the plane is stale. All around me, people are sleeping—breath, bodies, hopes, dreams.

I could have been many things in this lifetime. I never set out to be a pianist. It was Gurevicius who set me on the path. I can't imagine any other life now. If something happened to my hands or eyes, I have no idea what I'd do. Often, I feel luckier than I deserve. People ask, "Don't you get tired of playing the same music that's been played all those hundreds of years?" I don't.

But the reviews are often hard. It hardly matters whether they're good or bad. A few months back, a music critic in *The Times* complimented me on the "elasticity and lightness" of my playing. Someone else, reviewing a different concert, wrote about my understanding of the "darker hues" of music. Even when the reviewers are positive, I can find ways to make myself feel bad. *What does he mean by "darker hues?" Is my playing depressing to people?* I was happy, though, about a recent one. "Ms. Korczak delivered an expressive, nuanced performance on Friday night. Her passion and personal involvement with the music created an intimate, powerful experience."

It's all ego. What I really want is to give something of value to people, something they can use in their lives; I want my intention to be heard accurately. I'd like to think I'll outlive the desire to please, that in time, I'll stop reading reviews altogether and ask myself only whether I gave it everything I had.

I used to practice on an upright, and my father thought I should have something better. The Steinway had sat for years in a partially heated room in Grand Island. The damper pedal didn't work, and it needed new felts, but the sounding board was perfect. My father had it moved to New York and paid to have someone fix it. It's turned out to be a first-rate instrument. I adore this piano. The action is responsive, the bass has oomph, and the tone in the upper register is clear and sweet and expressive. When the piano movers brought it up the three flights of stairs, I was so scared, one of them told me to go out on the front steps and sit down, they couldn't handle both me and a grand piano. They moved it to a spot in the living room near the window. When I sat down to play, the ground danced under the damper pedal, the music moved through my blood and out the top of my head and through the roof and into the sapphire-singing sky.

In Bieńkówka, I used to cross the road every day to visit Władysław. *Ho!* he'd say, his head wobbling with joy. Before the war, he wasn't allowed to go outdoors; but after his father and brothers left, his mother began taking him out. She propped his feet on the little wooden shelf of his wheelchair, one foot flat, the other twisted over. She bumped him down the stoop and out onto the dirt road that wound between the houses in our village. His hands, with their big knuckles, rested on his knees. He blinked and smiled into the leaves. On some days, he was so happy, light seemed to shine from him.

One rainy day, sheets of water swept across the river. I ran across the road and knocked on his door. In the parlor, a great crack divided the plaster wall. Horsehair stuck out of it like whiskers. Mrs. Mikołajzyck wheeled Władysław in, moved a chair next to him and held a bowl of porridge in her lap. He made gobbling sounds, his tongue was everywhere. I had to look away. But then he was finished. His mother wiped his mouth on his blue towel, went to the kitchen and came back with an accordion I'd never seen before. A double-sided eagle sat above a row of buttons. When Władysław heard the first notes, he rocked with joy. His mouth opened, and great cries came from him.

W murowanej piwnicy, his mother sang.

Harawck! Harawck! he roared.

The morning it happened, I was in school. Later, his mother, crying hysterically, told us that an army truck had passed them on the road, then backed up.

A couple of German soldiers got out and asked his name.

Władysław, Mrs. Mikołajczyk said. *His name is Władysław.*

How old is he? the soldier asked in German.

Nineteen.

What's wrong with him?

Nothing. Nothing is wrong. He is good Polish boy. He is best boy ever was.

I can see her standing there in the middle of the

road, dread girdling her belly, pulling her breath tighter, Władysław in his chair, his head tilted, looking up at the man in the odd cap. Perhaps he smiled his lopsided grin.

They yanked the blue towel from his hands and loaded him into the back of the truck. The last Mrs. Mikołajczyk saw of him, his knees were crumpled under him. His fists were over his eyes. For days, she searched for him. Finally she gave up. We didn't see her for a week, and then she sat on the front steps of her house and unraveled all the sweaters she'd ever knitted. It was cold, the wind was blowing. My mother tried to bring her inside, but she shrugged her off, heaps of bumpy wool around her ankles.

My childhood all but ended when they took him away. There were moments when I was still a girl, when I hung from the handle of the water pump, when I ran up onto the stone revetment and watched the ferry cross the river. But after he disappeared, happiness was never just happiness again. I can see his smile, the thread of drool falling onto his blue towel. I can't bear to think how they might have broken him.

13

The flight attendants have turned the lights low; a movie's started. On the screen, a man leaps from a cliff into a river. His pursuers stand high over the water and watch to see where he surfaces. Across the aisle, the baby begins to cry. Her mother is holding her with one arm and digging in a bag with the other. The priest next to me opens his eyes. He looks around, glances at the flickering movie screen, and begins to talk.

"I'm glad to have left your country for good," he says.

"It's only half my country," I say. "I was born in Poland."

He ignores this. "I will never come back to the United States, not for anything."

"Why?"

"You want to know? I was at the Blessed Immaculate Conception Heart of Mary Seminary, St. Louis, Missouri. I was very happy to be studying there, the only foreign scholarship student. I wished to celebrate the mysteries of Christ and the Liturgy of the Hours faithfully, to live peaceably with my brothers.

"But my fellow students played impractical jokes on me. I do not know why. I did nothing to harm them. They knew I am very fearful of frogs, and they put the frogs in my food, in my bed, in the bathroom when they knew I was on the point of going there. I made an appointment with the Dean to say that it was insupportable being a scrapegoat day in, day out, and do you know what he said to me? He told me that God was testing my commitment, that in the life I had chosen I would need to be open to God's word, however He chose to manifest Himself. He told me that with earnest prayer, my fear could be overcome. I tried earnestly for several weeks and went back to see the Dean when it was clear that prayer was not efficacious. He then told me that my fears were unnatural and suggested I go to see a counselor.

"I did do so, even though I did not believe he could do anything for me. I was quite right. The counselor did something to me called neuro linguistic programs and told me to imagine the frogs were angels.

"Two nights before we were to receive our Master of Divinity degree, I had been visiting with another Indian student from St. Louis University. I came back quite late from dinner, opened the door of my room, and there were frogs everywhere. They had defecated on my books, on the floor, on the bed. My fellow students came out of their rooms to watch what would happen. I was very angry. I ran at them with a stick. I managed to strike several of them around their heads and shoulders, the ones who were fat and couldn't run fast.

"There was a question of whether the authorities would allow me to receive my degree. They were questioning my psychological health. I was bestowed the degree in the end although I did not attend the ceremony.

"I find your countrymen very odd people. These men were candidates for the priesthood. They were the chosen. They said I was a Hindu, not a Christian. They said I worshipped gods with many arms."

"They were very ignorant."

"Yes, you are right."

"Still, you're finished now, and you'll never need to go back."

"No." He looks relieved to have spoken. He pulls the blanket up around his neck, closes his eyes, and soon his breath grows gentle and even.

Eemo is with Ichiro now. Before going out to Nebraska for what turned out to be the last visit with my father, I went next door. "I've got a favor to ask you," I said when Ichiro answered. "A big one."

"Why don't you come in? Do you want some coffee?"

"Just half a cup."

He opened a door to a kitchen cupboard. He took out two cups and set them on the counter. "I forget, do you take anything?"

"Just black, thanks."

He passed me a cup and indicated a chair in the corner of the kitchen beside a small table. He brought in a chair from the other room and sat down. "So, tell me." The way he said it was so kind, I felt like casting all my burdens on his lap. I told him I had to visit my father who was sick.

"Yes?"

And that unfortunately, Peter and Margot, Eemo's two usual caretakers, were both going to be out of town.

"I know nothing about birds," he said. "I'm afraid I might hurt him."

"He's more likely to hurt you."

"Why? What does he do?"

"You know what?" I said, "I'll call the Vet and see if he knows of someone."

"Why don't I meet him, and see how it goes?"

"I should have thought to call the Vet to begin with."

"How about Tuesday?"

"Really, I wish I hadn't asked."

A few days later, Ichiro and I stood outside the door to my apartment. "Usually he does better if you let him make the first move," I told him.

"You mean I let him bite me first."

I laughed. "Seriously though, you mustn't ever put your hand in his cage. And if you decide to do this, I definitely wouldn't let him out. He'd dive bomb your head, and you'd never get him back in. He often paces and shrieks. Or he might huddle in one place. If he doesn't go on a hunger strike, he should eat anything you do. There should always be seed and water in his cage. I give him a stalk of sorghum every morning for a treat. He adores Cheerios. And fruit and vegetables. Any kind of Chinese or Thai food."

Ichiro walked over to the cage while Eemo eyed him coldly. His neck ruff puffed with disdain; he sidled along his perch, then levered himself up the side of the cage using his beak as a fulcrum, hung upside down, and made his way across the top and down the other side.

"Just ignore him," I said, turning my back. Eemo began to bawl and roar.

"Don't do that!" said Ichiro, turning to face him.

"Rawwckk!" Eemo yelled.

"Better to leave us alone," he said.

I left the room. There was more shrieking and roaring, a volley of *not my faults*, more bad-tempered bawling. I almost went in and said, "Forget it." But then came a one-fingered rendition of *Twinkle, Twinkle, Little Star* on the piano. The tune kept repeating. All at once, there was Eemo yodeling over the top. When I came in to tell Ichiro dinner was served, the two of them were eye to eye, Ichiro bent over Eemo's cage. "Your vibrato needs work, pal," he said.

"Mr. Rogers haha?"

"What's he talking about?"

"It's his private joke. It sounds as if you've passed muster." I moved Eemo's cage into the kitchen and speared an apple onto his fruit peg.

Ichiro said, "Well, I'm willing to give it a try." He turned to Eemo. "You and me, buddy. We're going to have lots of wild parties while she's gone."

That night, he talked about his great-grandfather who'd left Yokohama in the 1890s to work on a sugar plantation in Hawaii. He told me he still had the long knife his grandfather used for killing wild pigs in the great gulches of Kauai. His grandmother was a picture bride from Japan.

"Did they stay married?"

"Sixty-one years, until she died."

"I can't imagine staying married that long."

"I thought I'd be married as long as I lived," he said.

"What happened?"

"It didn't work out."

I waited. "Do you want to say anything more?"

"No." He blotted his mouth with a napkin. "Not now."

He left shortly afterwards.

14

The man with the big head has gone to the bathroom. His wife is slumped toward a stranger in the window seat. It's midnight, New York time. At my feet is a cloth bag. Inside is a cardboard box, and inside the box is a black plastic box that contains all that's left of my father. If I can't part with his ashes in Bieńkówka, I'll bring them back home. I'd say it's fifty-fifty. The crematorium people call what's in this box "cremains". It's one of the uglier made-up words I've ever heard.

Two days before I left Eemo with Ichiro, the phone rang. "Nadia?" said Maria. "She call me yesterday."

"Who?"

"Linda Kopecky. She has something to say. I don't know why she want."

"Do you want me to come with you?"

There was silence.

"You want me to meet you at the Red Cross?"

"Yes, please."

"I have students until two. Is three o'clock okay?"

"Yes. I think is okay."

"How are you doing?"

"I don't sleep too good last night."

She was waiting outside the building when I came up the street, her hair combed back with water. A lavender vein at her temple throbbed.

"You're limping," I said.

"Something wrong with my knee, I don't know."

I squeezed her hand. "How's Pootsie?"

"Okay. No problem."

"Do you want me to go in with you or wait in the waiting room?"

"Come in. Of course."

The receptionist said Linda Kopecky was still tied up. We sat down in the same chairs we'd sat in when we'd first met. A voice came out of one of the inner offices, and Maria leaned over toward me. "That's the one," she whispered. "Linda Kopecky. My caseworker. If she says you can't come in, you say I'm your *ciotka*."

"You *are* my auntie, aren't you?"

Maria smiled, the first time that day. But right away, her face went dark.

I reached over and touched her hands. "You want my sweater? You're freezing."

"No. No problem." Maria picked up a magazine and riffled through the pages as though she was in a beauty parlor. She looked up. "My husband was very good with the horses, did I tell you? And his father. But he say I don't know nothing, I don't even know never go behind a horse."

A door opened. "Mrs. Horowitz?"

I introduced myself.

"She is coming with me," said Maria.

We followed Linda Kopecky to an office with a small window. An ivy plant was in its last throes. Ms. Kopecky was a large woman with big hands who gave the impression of not being strong. Her hair was dyed reddish blond and showed dark at the roots; her eyes were deeply shaded with fatigue. Her lipstick was too orange for her face. She shook Maria's hand. "Please," she said, gesturing to a chair for each of us and sitting down at her desk. We crowded in, knee to knee.

"We heard earlier this week from the tracing service," said Linda Kopecky. "They've turned up a Jacob Horowitz in Łódź whose age matches your husband's. We need your permission to go the next step."

Maria held her hands clasped tight under her breasts. Ms. Kopecky waited. Maria's hands began to shake, and then her head.

I reached over and put my hand on her knee.

"Do we have your permission to get in touch with Mr. Horowitz?"

"It is not my Jacob," said Maria. "It is not the right one."

"How do you know?"

"I know, is all. I know. That is not his place, Łódź."

"Many people relocated after the war," said Ms. Kopecky gently. "They went to places they never would have gone before. He could have been trying to find work. Or his village might not have been safe. He could have been looking for you."

"He would not go to Łódź to find me."

"Perhaps you'd like some time to let the information settle in. It's hard when you've been hoping for so long."

"I do not have hope now. He is not the one." She raised her voice. "This is not the right man, I'm telling you."

"When you come on Tuesday, we can talk again," said Ms. Kopecky. "You've been waiting a long time, Maria. It doesn't make sense to stop now, when we think we might have located him."

"Maybe he has different wife now."

"That does happen sometimes."

"My Jacob is in Tykocin. He isn't going to Łódź. He doesn't even know Łódź."

"We'll talk about it again next Tuesday, what do you say?"

"Maybe I don't come Tuesday. I tell you my Jacob is not going to Łódź. You don't hear what I'm telling you."

"Do you want to go home and think it over?" I asked.

"Yes, I want to go home now." Maria picked her purse off the floor and stood up. "Did he have children and a wife, this man?"

"I don't know," Ms. Kopecky said. "We can't go the next step without your permission." As we left, she was standing by the ivy, her hands dangling.

Out on the street, I said to Maria, "How could you do that after all the time she's spent on this? You don't have any idea whether he's the right one or not."

"I know, is all." Her bottom lip quivered.

"Let's go get a cup of coffee. You want a cup of coffee, and maybe something to eat? Come on, we'll have an early dinner if you're hungry, you won't have to cook...Are you hungry?"

"No. Just coffee."

We stopped in a little place furnished with red walls and

huge mirrors. When we sat down, I could see the front and back of Maria's head at the same time. She sat shrunk into herself, wringing the handle of her purse. She buttoned the top button of her coat.

"What do you take in your coffee?"

"Cream and sugars," she said. "Four sugars."

The red walls of the coffee shop throbbed. I disappeared out of one mirror and appeared in another. I bought the coffees, poured cream and the sugars into Maria's, but when I returned to our table, she was gone, as though she'd slipped into one of the mirrors. I sat down and put a cup at Maria's place.

Anything could have happened in forty-nine years. Jacob could have remarried, he could have turned selfish and dandruffy and mean-spirited. If he turned out to be the right one, where would they live? Out of the corner of my eye, I caught sight of a figure in a mirror, but when I looked directly, it had disappeared. Something like birds flew up into the reflection and settled back out of sight. The mirrors made me mistrust my eyes, as though they'd gone out of whack the way my father's once did.

He and I were talking on the phone when his end went quiet.

"What?" I asked.

"My mother's in the barn milking Lucja," he said. "I see the milk pail. She has on the yellow apron and is wearing my father's coat and her rubber boots that come up to her knees. I'm not remembering, I actually *see* it. Like my brain stored it. I see the barn here, right before me. My mother is in the room right here, right now."

"What's happening now?"

"Some men are loading goods onto a ship. Now they're gone."

Like that, the mirrors stored other worlds. I stood up and went to the door and looked up and down the street for Maria and came back to the table. She'd left her gloves behind but had taken her coat and purse. Was she upset enough to wander into traffic? I stood up again and went to the woman behind the counter. "Excuse me, did you happen to see the person who was with me? An older woman in a plaid coat?"

"She's in the ladies' room."

The ladies room, of course. I went back to the table and had a sip of coffee. It was very bad. I took my cup over to the coffee station and added cream. A shadow moved in the mirror. When I looked, there was my own hat, black velvet with a rhinestone. I turned. Maria was back. Her forehead was so white it looked powdered. Her nose was thin and pinched, some wildness in her face.

"I'm thinking it could be him," she said. "But say this is the right Jacob Horowitz. Okay. But I don't know him no more. He don't know me. So what I think is this. If Jacob is in Łódź, it is not my Jacob. Too much time is over."

"You don't want to know for sure?" I asked.

"No," said Maria. With the mirror inches from the back of her, she moved her head violently to one side.

We finished our coffee, and I hugged her goodbye at the subway. Her hair had settled flat against her head except for one bit sticking out by her ear. I tucked it down and kissed her on the cheek.

"Nelson," said Eemo mournfully when I came in the door.

"Who the hell is Nelson anyway?" I said. "Why are you always moping around about Nelson? We don't know anyone by that name!"

Eemo cocked his head and reached his foot slowly, thoughtfully, up to his ear hole and ran it back and forth. "Bird-o?"

When he'd settled down with a stalk of sorghum, I called Maria. "Did you get home okay?" I asked.

"Yes."

"I'm sorry," I said.

"It's okay."

"What will you have for supper tonight?"

"Chicken."

"That sounds good."

"Pootsie is here, eating his dinner."

"How is he?"

"Okay."

There was silence. "You know, I've been thinking, it could be my Jacob."

"Do you want to know?"

She was quiet on her end a moment. "Yes. I must know."

"Do you want me to come back with you next week?"

"No, no. I go like always. They say, you know, never chase the wind in the field. It's no good to try to find."

"But you have to know," I said.

"It's the truth."

"I'll pray for the best."

"You know," she said, "after I leave Poland, they arrest me and take me to Foehrenwald, displaced person camp. I don't think I tell you this part. Did I tell you?"

"No."

"And one time there are some Jews who come and do a show. American Jews. His name is Herman Yablokoff. It is first time I laugh in how long, and I think if Jacob is dead, otherwise I must come to America, because here is where people laugh...Are you crying, Nadi? Don't cry. It's okay."

"I love you, Maria."

"It's okay, everything's okay."

"I love you," I said again. "Be good to yourself."

"Me too. *Do widzenia.* You're good friend," said Maria. "Best in world."

I put down the phone. How many people live like Maria? Here and not here.

A five-thousand-year-old Iceman was found in a glacier in the Italian Alps, perfectly preserved. It gave me a queer feeling, thinking about his eyelashes here in the present, when they shouldn't have been here at all. The Iceman had been killed, attacked from behind. An arrowhead was embedded in his shoulder. Next to him was a longbow, arrow shafts, a dagger, pieces of antler for making arrows. In his stomach was his last meal, undigested pollen from a plant that blossoms in the springtime. He was wearing a loin cloth, goatskin leggings, a hide coat, shoes, a grass cape. The people who unburied him would have smelled his animal smell.

The day they took Jacob, he would have smelled of the horses he shod.

When they found the Iceman, they thought he was in Austria. But later, it turned out he'd been found a hundred meters inside Italy. How little he would have cared for national boundaries.

Jacob was Polish. If he'd been born somewhere else, he and Maria could have finished out their lives together. Their

daughter would be a grown woman now, maybe with children of her own. If my mother and I had missed the truck
that took us to Slovakia, we might have died along with
my grandmother. If we'd gone to Paris instead of Lyons,
we might have been killed in the bombing. Lives stretch
forward on a string of ifs.

15

I was astounded when I hugged my father, how rattle-boned his body had become in such a short time. Tricia had him by one elbow, helping him to stand. "What's up?" I asked.

"Nothing much." He lowered his voice to a growl. "You're too thin, baby. What are you eating?"

"You're a fine one to talk." I helped him sit back down in his favorite chair, and Tricia disappeared into the kitchen.

"Did you plant the seeds?" I asked.

"I don't even know why I ordered them. Trish planted the spinach. She likes it—I seem to recall that Russian of yours liking it too."

"Probably still does."

"Do you ever see him?"

"We talked on the phone last week."

"It's what I always said, never trust a Russian."

Trish poked her head in the door to say she was leaving for the day.

"Bye, sweetheart," my father said. "Take a coupla days off while Nadia's here. I'll pay you just the same."

She waved goodbye.

"Peter's not Russian," I said when she'd left. "He grew up in New York."

"It doesn't matter where they grow up, it's in the blood."
He let forth a volley that I'd heard a number of times before, almost to the word. "Those bastards, they sat across
the river in 1944 and watched Warsaw burn. Goddamned
lying sons-of-bitches. They encouraged the Poles to rise up
and said they'd be right behind them."

"Peter didn't have anything to do with that."

"Well, he pretended he was with you when he was seeing someone else, didn't he?"

"I was half responsible for what happened."

"You were seeing someone too?"

"That's not what I mean."

"I rest my case."

"How about a cup of coffee?"

"You know what I'd really like?" he said.

"What?"

"A drive somewhere."

"It's not too much?"

"I've been sitting on my goddamn duff for weeks."

"You want something to drink before we go?"

"Too much trouble." He worked his legs off the bed,
and I helped him with his pants, pulled socks over his feet,
and tied his shoes.

"How about the bathroom?"

"I guess we'd better." We made our way down the hall,
four feet shuffling, through the door to the toilet. I hesitated about whether to stay or go, but I helped him pull down
his pants and held him around the waist. I felt embarrassed
for him, his old puckered self, but he didn't seem to think
anything of it. There are things you tell yourself you could
never do, but then you do them and you wonder why you
ever thought you couldn't. I helped him zip his trousers,

and we tottered out to the car.

Getting behind the wheel, I asked, "Where to?"

"How about we head for Alda first? Get off 281 as soon as we can." He meant dirt roads. Open fields. I put the car in gear, and soon we were rattling along ruler-straight roads, over corrugations, sliding sideways in sand. I could feel him relax next to me. Huge fields of plowed soil took our eyes out to the horizon and beyond. Ten-mile-high sky, all the sky you'd ever want. To our right, a huge irrigation device stretched across a field, like the wings of a pterodactyl. A tractor pulled a tank of nitrogen toward the horizon. Once upon a time, after he quit foundry work, my father did this sort of fertilizing; he set the huge irrigation arms and ran the combine harvesters. He called it factory work. His kind of farming, you got your hands in the dirt.

We passed a patch of winter wheat coming up green. Every now and then, a group of cottonwoods punctuated the loneliness; and then there was the ghost of a one-room school house slumped to one side, an outhouse behind it. My father's hand pointed out two birds in the air. The sand-hill cranes were back, necks outstretched, long legs trailing. Small groups on the ground fed under the stalks of last year's corn. I pulled off the road, cut the engine, and opened the door. From a distance, we heard the birds murmuring to each other—*garoo—a-a-a*. From somewhere close by came the sound of a meadowlark.

"Mom loved that sound."

I turned and saw his face change as he looked out at the field. "Fifty-five years I've been here," he said. "Who would've imagined I'd end up here?"

"Are you sorry?"

He looked at me as though I was crazy. "What's there to

be sorry about? I'm surprised is all." He began to cough and couldn't stop. "Give me a whack," he sputtered.

I thumped him on his back while the cranes moved closer to the car.

"Aren't they something?" my father said softly.

"Do you remember when you and Mom and I went out to the river to see them?"

"Sure I do," he said.

My father had wanted to tramp into the nesting site on our own. *Those damn bird tours are for foreigners*, he'd said. *What do you think you are*? my mother had said. She got us a space on an Audubon tour, and we woke at 3:30 in the morning, met the group leader in a parking lot, and drove to the river in a caravan of cars. When we opened the car door, the sound was like a football stadium erupting. There were so many birds and the sound was so immense, you couldn't hold it all inside. *I'll be damned*, my father kept saying under his breath. *I'll be damned*.

The leader led us to a bunker in the dark, covered on the river side with burlap, slits cut out for viewing. My father, for once, was speechless. In the half light, the birds looked like lily pads in the shallow river. As the sun rose, hundreds, thousands, revealed themselves, almost as tall as people. They walked through the water, preened, high-stepped, held their enormous wings out from their bodies, leapt in the air, twirled. Two by two, three by three, they flew off to their feeding grounds for the day.

I started up the car and turned to my father. "Ready to keep going?"

Six, seven, eight miles we drove, with only one abandoned house all that way. I imagined coming back and taking pictures of the house and the one down the road from my father's and others like them. All the lives lived in those kitchens and lonely bedrooms, the prairie winds blowing through them, blowing and blowing. I imagined people who'd gone mad listening to that wind. Through the corner of my eye, I saw him glance toward me.

"I need to ask you something," he said.

"Want me to pull over?"

"Why don't you."

I drove to the top of a small rise, halfway down the other side, and parked. I passed him the bottle of water. He held it in two hands and took a swig. And then he opened the door, struggled to his feet and stood by the side of the road unsteadily, hanging onto the car while the wind roared around him. I joined him, holding him up on the other side, and we looked out at the land surrounded by fence posts stretching before and behind us.

"So what's up?"

"When you give the chickens to Olly, could you do me a favor? Would you tell him I don't want any of them killed? I'll provide more than enough money for them to live out their days."

I looked at him, surprised, remembering the axe falling on the necks of chickens in Poland, my father so matter-of-fact, he might have been pulling a carrot from the garden.

"I know I'm a foolish old man."

I leaned over and kissed him. "There's nothing about you that's foolish."

"If I was going to be around a while, I'd turn into one of those tofu burger nuts."

Why not? He'd seen enough blood for seven lifetimes.

"One thing I don't mind eating though."

"What's that?"

"Goat…Son of a gun, look at that, all that topsoil blowing away. There's no excuse for plowing the way they do," my father said. "The soil is tired. Do you see how tired it looks?"

"Yes." He sounded tired too. I told him no one would harm a single feather on a single chicken's head. "How about a hot fudge sundae in Gibbon?"

"Sounds good."

I helped him back into the car and climbed into the driver's seat. We went along without talking a mile or two and then passed through a grove of trees, the only shade for miles. A pair of bluebirds flew up beside the car in a flash, so bright their wings looked made from sky.

16

I'm looking out into the darkness. If I squint, I can imagine the outlines of an ancient map, the land masses misshapen by ignorance. *Terra incognita. Dragons here.* I'm as ignorant of the country where my father has gone as those old map-makers were of the earth. Death will touch every person on this plane—the one unalterable law of life. Its breath will roll over each one of us, touching us like a dog's nose on a cold night, a single shock to the skin, familiar, almost domestic, wildness in the dark of its eyes. I can't imagine saying, the way my father did, I'm not afraid. I *am* afraid. I believe he was telling the truth, but how did he get there?

I lean my face closer to the window, rest my forehead against the coolness. In the last week I was with him, his eyes grew more distant by the day. They looked like coal miner eyes. It's been years since I thought of those miners—seven of them trapped underground in West Virginia, a ceiling of rock collapsed over them. On television, the first one my parents ever had, we watched the searchlights roaming over the hole, women with kerchiefs over their heads, children sunk into silence, the waiting families slapped up against cameras and microphones, the stretchers that took away the dead miners, the gaunt faces of the living men as they brought them out of the darkness. Their beards had grown, their eyes were flat, their lips cracked. They'd drunk their own urine, they'd licked moisture from the walls. Some of them walked into those bright lights, others were carried in the arms of their fellow miners. They tried to smile, they tried to pour their arms around their children. Their eyes looked like my father's when he returned from the war—the same eyes I saw in him that last week in Nebraska.

"When I was in Italy in the hospital," my father said over breakfast one morning, "there were men who couldn't talk. There was nothing wrong with them. They'd seen too much."

"You saw too much too," I said.

The wind rattled the windowpanes. "The war had to be fought," he said. "But when I think of this latest goddamn fiasco…that rich, greedy son-of-a-bitch after oil. And look what he left behind—his own soldiers poisoned by uranium."

Everything about Operation Desert Storm made me sick: the crude pretense of fighting a war for the freedom of Kuwait; the made-for-TV theatrics; the crowing over the surgical precision of our bombs. Hemingway said in modern war, *you will die like a dog for no good reason.* Exactly what happened to the 300 Iraqui civilians bombed in a bunker with one of those smart bombs.

"Did you know in World War II he bailed out of a plane," my father continued, "and left two of his crew to go down in flames?"

"Who are you talking about?"

"George H.W. Bush, of course. That's what he's made of. In the war, you better believe, men in the Polish Air Force protected one another. They looked after their allies and countrymen, not just their own asses. It's called honor."

I went to the kitchen and returned with milk and shredded wheat. I could hear him muttering as I came back in the room. "This country's full of morons. I'm not so smart myself, but at least I know a lying bastard when I see one...He should never of been elected president in the first place.

"By the way," he said, changing the subject, "the hospice nurse came over the other day. I told her when I can't feed myself, that's it. I don't want anyone feeding me. She wanted to know about my loved ones, whether I'd let them know. 'I've only got one loved one,' I said, 'and she'll respect my wishes.'"

"You're right, I will." But what if he couldn't breathe? Was I going to just leave him to battle it out? I looked at him a moment, at his untidy eyebrows and fierce, gaunt eyes. I grabbed his mug and my own and went into the kitchen and set them down in the sink and leaned against the edge of the counter. Outside, the spinach Tricia had planted was coming up. I held my hands over my mouth and ran the water in the kitchen sink until I stopped crying.

All is change, all is impermanence, the Buddhists say. It's true, but right then, it didn't really help. Every day, my father was loosening his hold on the world. Standing there at the sink, I'd have done anything to make his last days happy. But all that came to me was food. *Stay a little longer. Eat.*

I went back with a cup of coffee. "I'm going to make us an Easter feast for tomorrow," I told him. "I'm going shopping after breakfast. Want anything?"

"Don't make a lot of trouble for yourself."

"It's no trouble." I cleared the dishes, helped him back to bed, and went out to his car. The cold was intense that morning, as though the inland sea still filled Nebraska. I've never found Nebraska to be all that habitable a place. People who live there greet each other heartily and slap each other on the back; they laugh in coffee shops, but it feels like underneath they're really saying, *Don't abandon me, for godsakes. Talk to me, laugh with me, anything but this wind.*

When we first came here, my mother sent me to a YWCA swim program. I didn't know anyone in the class. I couldn't swim and understood almost no English. The teacher, whose name was Chuck, smelled fear the way dogs do. *Ko-zack!!* he yelled. The name twisted off the tile walls and bounced back, hard and foreign.

"*My name is Korczak,* I told him, my voice shaking. I had to say it. My name was all I had.

I know what your name is, he yelled. *Now get in the pool!*

The other kids were already bobbing in the deep end. I started down the steps into the shallow end.

The other end!

I beg your pardon? I said. I had no idea what he was talking about.

Get in! he roared. *How many times do I have to tell you?*

I continued down the steps, and he turned his back and walked to the deep end and said something under his breath to one of the boys, and then louder, *Martin, show her how to get in.*

Martin came over to where I was. *Come here,* he said, not unkindly. He sounded as though he was going to be my friend. I climbed out and followed him to where the rest of the class were.

Like this, he said shoving me hard. I went under, came up, and went down again. My hands and legs thrashed. I heard laughter. Martin finally pulled me out. *You don't float, do you,* he said. I retched and threw up, but I didn't cry. I never let that bastard of a teacher see me cry. I turned my back on them all, ripped off my bathing cap, and walked to the locker room. I peeled off my suit and stuffed it in the swim bag and put on my clothes and went out into the bright street and thought of death.

I never felt safe in Nebraska after that. I suppose I could live there if I had to. But how? The flat land, the sky that dwarfs everything. I always felt ant-sized in Nebraska.

On the way to the market, I thought of all the things I'd make my father: *śledzie w śmietanie, zupa grzybowa, bigos.* Pork and beef and sauerkraut; juniper berries, apples, prunes simmering on the stove. *Buraczki po polsku. Pierogi* with cabbage and mushroom and potato fillings. Fruit compote and *szarlotka* for dessert. I left the store with three bags of groceries. And then on to the liquor store for vodka. When I returned home, my father's eyes were closed, the cup of coffee cold beside him. Out of his sleep, he muttered "*Która godzina? Zaczekaj chwilę…*" *What time is it? Wait a minute.* His hand was lying open on the quilt, a ropy vein standing out on the back of it. His cheeks were sunken and unshaven; his skin had a bluish tinge. For a moment, watching him, I thought, this is what it'll be like. Just like this, only he won't wake.

And then he did. "Are you leaving?" he said.

"I just got back."

"You get everything you need?"

"I bought us Żubrówka."

"Good girl."

"Can I ask you something? After Mama died, was there anything afterwards? I mean, did you ever hear from her?"

"Zero," he said. "I don't believe in that stuff."

I mixed the flour and salt for *pierogi*, and the eggs and water, and combined them with a fork. I rolled out the dough, punched out circles, put dollops of filling in each, folded them over and pressed the sides together into crescents. I heated a big pot of water, turned it down to simmer and dropped the *pierogi* in, about a dozen at a time.

The next day, we ate and ate. I felt like Maria. My father was eating more than he wanted, to please me.

"You've outdone yourself," he said, blotting his lips with a napkin. "I haven't had beets like those since I don't know when."

"How about a break?" I blew out the candles and took his elbow. "Are you in the mood for a nap?"

"No. No." He looked restless. "I'll just sit in bed."

I helped steer him into it, and when he caught his breath, he said, "You know, I wasn't any kind of hero during the war. I don't want you thinking that." He was staring at his hands as though he'd never seen them before. They were burned from his years in the foundry, small white scars over the backs and up his arms.

I said, too quietly, "I don't know about the war. But I do know the rest."

"I can't hear you, speak up!"

I raised my voice. "What I'm saying is you left Poland, you learned to speak a foreign language, you made a comfortable, happy life for us. If that didn't take courage, I'd like to know what did."

He shrugged. "I'm glad you see it that way."

"I'm going to open the vodka. Do you want apple cake

with it?"

"You bet."

I went to leave the room, but he called me back. "Do you remember this song? *If I knew you were comin' I'd've baked a cake, Howd-ya do, howd-ya do, howd-ya do.*"

I smiled. "You shoulda been on Broadway, Pop." I left the room, went into the kitchen, and picked up the bottle of vodka. I wanted to smash it over the side of the counter, break something, anything. I poured myself a couple of fingers and downed it. I drank a little more. *Last time, last time,* the voice in my head said. I took two plates down from the cupboard and cut a slice of cake for each of us. Back in his room, I poured vodka for us both.

"It's the real thing," he said, sniffing it. "*Na zdrowie!*" We klinked, and he drank deeply.

I knocked my glass back. "More?"

"Sure. But first, I need to pee." He set down the empty glass, and I helped him swivel his legs off the bed and stand. I held his elbow, and we made the trek to the bathroom and back. He lay down and caught his breath.

"Why don't I come back again next week?" I said.

"What about your work?"

"I could find people to fill in."

"*Nie przejmuj się.*" Don't worry. "Trish keeps me going pretty good. You'll come back in a month or so, I don't want you disrupting your life."

"*To dla mnie nie ma znaczenia.*" It's not important to me. Not right now.

"*I* care about it." He took a deep breath. "You made a good life for yourself, honey, you should be proud. Living in New York. Playing all that difficult music in front of hundreds of people."

"Thanks, *Tatuś*. I'm used to it. It doesn't feel that hard."

"When's your next big concert?"

"Not for a few weeks. We're doing Brahms. I think they're recording it. I'll send you a copy if you'd like."

"Sure." His eyes grew cloudy. "Anyway, you go, it's all right." He drained his glass.

Years ago, my father taught me to polka. I couldn't have been more than seven or eight. He bent his knees low to bring himself closer to my height. He put my hands on his shoulders and his hands on my back. "*Odchyl się, odchyl się!*" *Lean out, lean out!*

We drank more than a half bottle between us that night. Mostly he talked about the war, making up for lost time—the subject was always off limits with my mother. He kept apologizing to me, but he couldn't stop. A barn full of dead horses. Fields burned black. The whine of bombers. *You saw their faces before they died. You don't forget that.*

Before I kissed him goodnight, my father said, "You be good to yourself now. You hear me?" He wasn't talking about tomorrow or next week. It was the closest he came to a goodbye. We were both drunk. I could hardly get him to the bathroom that one last time without us both falling on the floor where the hallway took a right turn.

Outside, the next morning, the taxi driver leaned on the horn. I wrapped my arms around my father and held him. "Better get out of here," he said. "You'll miss your plane." He stood hanging onto the frame of the front door. I turned back, and he lifted his hand.

17

I slept most of the way to New York. Night had already fall-en as the cab wove its way into the city. Outside the win-dow, a man pulled a wire shopping cart behind him. A truck engine roared beside us at a light. And then I was in the foyer on 102nd Street with its 1920s shabby marble. I dragged my suitcase upstairs and set it down outside the door, let myself in with the keys, and took off my hat and coat.

I wandered over to the piano bench, touched the keys, and played the simplest Mozart sonata of all, in C major. It's like a brook—youthful, and full of hope. I came to the end of the first movement and played it again, and then a third time. Finally, I went next door. Ichiro opened the door, and I hugged him like a child, feeling the music still in me. "I've brought you something," I said. I opened half an egg carton onto maroon, pink, and turquoise eggs.

"Where'd you get these?"

"My father raises exotic chickens."

"You've got an exotic chicken waiting for you."

"It went all right?" I asked.

"He screamed the first two days."

"And then he stopped?"

"More or less."

"You've had a lot of fun."

"We're good pals now. I taught him *Way Down Upon the Sewanee River*. He carries a pretty good tune." Eemo heard my voice from the other room and began shrieking.

"Is that my little bamboozle?"

"Hello Eemo, Hello Eemo," he said, spreading his tail.

I opened the door of his cage, held out my arm and kissed his beak. "Look at you. What a mess you are. Why do you pull out your pretty green feathers?"

"Nelson," he said, frumping.

"Who's Nelson anyway?" asked Ichiro.

"Some guy he talks about when he wants to tell you how miserable he is." I rubbed Eemo's toes. "Look at these little horny feet." Eemo looked down to where my finger was, and I kissed one foot, and then he was on my shoulder sidling up and down, up to my head, a little nuzzle, down to the top of my arm. But all at once, he started for Ichiro, a nasty look in his eye.

"*Nawet nie próbuj!*" I yelled. Don't even think about it! I put him back in his cage. "You little savage."

"...How's your father?"

"Not so good."

"You want to take it easy the next few days."

"Right." I cut him off, not wanting to cry.

"Here I'll get that for you," he said. He picked up the cage and followed me. Inside my place, he said, "Where does it go?"

"Just by the piano, thank you."

"I'll leave you to get settled. Goodbye, Eemo, old fellow. You've been a fine guest for the most part." He gave a small bow. "I'd be happy to take him again, Nadia. All you need to do is ask." He was turning to leave, when he said,

"I hope you know I'd do anything I could to help right now. Don't feel you have to be brave and you can't knock on my door."

The room began to swim. I thanked him, and he left.

I sat in the living room a long time, thinking. There was a time when I'd returned from Nebraska just like tonight— only it was my mother who was dying. I'd been out there for two weeks, cooking, cleaning, pretending she was going to recover. My father and I both knew better, but we couldn't talk about it until the last hour before I left.

All I wanted when I got home was for Peter to take care of me. He came back an hour or so after I did, talking fast, full of a lecture he'd just given. Brain whizzing, I used to call it. Finally, he seemed to notice I was there. "You've still got your hat on," he said.

"I was hoping you'd take me out for a bite to eat." He forgot to ask about my mother, so I told him. His eyes wandered.

I never wanted to feel disappointed in Peter. When I was young, I believed there'd be love in my life that would shake my bones and make me happy and keep shaking me, that this is what I was in the world for. But loving Peter came to something smaller than I'd imagined. Not that I didn't love him, but it was a broom closet of love rather than a big ballroom kind of love. I felt foolish even thinking it, but I wanted to come home to someone who told me that I was the most beautiful woman in the world.

"Shall we go to that Tibetan place?" he asked.

"I don't mind." Peter and I walked arm in arm down Columbus. The breeze was blowing straight off the river, brackish and raw.

"How's your article coming?" Peter was working with

two colleagues—a German and a Chinese man—on gravitational wave interactions and the Einstein-Rosen bridge.

"Good, good."

In front of us, a spaniel who'd lost the use of his back legs dragged himself forward with his two front legs. His paralyzed behind was strapped onto a little cart with wheels.

"I can't believe that," Peter said.

"What?"

"Think of the money that's gone into that dog—you could feed a family of four half a year on what's been spent."

"Do you suppose if the dog weren't alive, that family of four would ever see the money?"

"Nadia, it's people like that woman who create the inequities in the world."

"For heaven's sakes, that woman and her dog?"

"It's the mentality: I can have anything I want, I can use any resource available to me. That's how people think."

"Peter," I pleaded, "let's just walk, I can't think about this right now. I'm tired."

"You don't think about these things when you're not tired."

"I think about other things. Maybe I think about things you don't think about." I knew I should stop there, but I couldn't. We were no longer arm in arm. "I don't insist you think about what I think about. I detest mind-tyranny." We kept on, Peter hunched over as though I'd rained blows on his head.

Soon we were in front of the little restaurant. Inside, a waiter gave us a seat under an orange silk banner with Tibetan lettering on it. Under it, an English translation read, *Life is precious*. A tiny flame struggled from the wick of an oil lamp on the table. I looked up and muttered, "Life *is* precious." I reached across the table and took Peter's hand.

"What do you want to eat?" He eased his hand out of mine.

I glanced at the menu. "Why don't you order for us both?" Looking at Peter made me want to cry, how he'd come home all windblown and happy, and then everything was ruined. Was it me? Over and over, things collapsed like that with us.

After saying goodbye to Ichiro, I poured myself a glass of vodka, downed it, and had another. I was thinking that the only couple I knew whose love didn't slide toward indifference were my parents. Was it the years of being apart that made their years together what they were? I was about to pour myself a third glass when I stopped, needing to get out and shake off the trip.

I had my hand on the knob of the outer door when the shape of someone appeared outside the door.

I cried out.

"Just me," Ichiro said, opening the door.

"God almighty, I've lost ten years off my life."

"Sorry," he said.

"...Do you want to come out for a walk? I can't sleep."

He hesitated a moment and put his hat back on. He held the door, followed me out, and then made an odd, sort of protective motion. I looked down, noticed another of the mystery sculptures, and stopped.

I looked at him closely. "It's *you* who makes these, isn't it?"

"Yes."

"Why didn't you say so the first time?"

"I didn't want you to know. I like them just to appear.

A small something that a passerby might take home." He pushed his glasses up his nose.

"Did you do this where you lived before?"

"People often destroyed them in Brooklyn. I'd find them on the sidewalk. Now they disappear.

"I told you I don't like clutter, but I've always liked scavenging. I have a rule: I don't go looking for anything in particular. Whatever I find dictates what I make; whatever I don't use that week goes back in the trash."

I crouched down and peered at the small metal figure with the battered helmet and shield, leaning on a pike. The eyes were tiny Phillips screws, set in at an angle. A washer, bent and scarred, formed the helmet. Ichiro had shaped tin cans for armor and left half a label from a Del Monte pineapple can. A sign was tucked between the arm and the shield, barely legible in the street light:

> HAVING CLEANED HIS ARMOUR, TURNED HIS STEEL CAP INTO A HELMET, BAPTIZED HIS NAG AND CONFIRMED HIMSELF, THE ONLY REMAINING TASK WAS TO FIND A LADY OF WHOM HE COULD BE ENAMOURED. FOR A KNIGHT ERRANT WITHOUT A LADY-LOVE IS A TREE WITHOUT LEAVES OR FRUIT, A BODY WITHOUT A SOUL.
>
> --Miguel de Cervantes

"I'd like you to take him," he said.

"I couldn't."

"Why not?" He smiled. "I made him with you in mind."

I didn't know what to say.

"I thought maybe you needed a protector."

"I've got Eemo," I said, not very graciously.

He looked amused, what I could see of his face.

"Shall we walk?"

We went along in silence for half a block until he said, "You know, you don't have to be scared of me."

"I'm not scared of you."

"I think you are, a little."

"How do you know how I feel?"

"I don't."

"Well, you're right, I *am* a little scared of you. Not you really. I've been thinking of Peter, my second husband. All that hope and affection we began with grew thinner and thinner over time. I found it very discouraging. I still do. I never want any part of that again. Do you remember when we were eating soup and I asked you why you hadn't stayed married? And you didn't answer? I don't usually ask those kinds of questions, but I imagine you experienced something similar with your wife."

We rounded the corner.

"That wasn't what happened," he said, slowing his pace. "I once had two daughters. The oldest, Yuriko, drowned on the south shore of Cape Cod. Harumi and I were both there when it happened. She'd be twenty-seven next month."

"I'm so sorry."

"I appreciate it." We walked in silence a few steps before he continued. "All the things that people say about losing a child are true. Harumi and I tried not to let it drive us apart; but we only stayed together five more years. Miyu, our other daughter, was seven when we divorced."

"I'm really sorry."

He clasped his hands behind his back and leaned forward a little as he walked. "Our marriage ended slowly, but at the time, it felt quite sudden. We were vacationing in the mountains, and there was a storm one night. Harumi was frightened and wanted to go home, but I persuaded her to stay until morning. At daybreak, we went out to pack the car and found it dented with hail. In an unguarded moment, she looked at me with such bitterness—as though I could have prevented it. I knew we were finished."

"Because she blamed you?"

"And I blamed her too. I wasn't big enough to admit that our daughter's death was as much my fault as hers. I'd been facing away from the water when it happened. But in fact, I'd been living carelessly for years. Careless toward my wife and daughters, careless in my work."

"Most people live that way."

"But I've been punished differently than most." He said it without self-pity. We were on Broadway and 105th, heading back toward 102nd. Ahead of us, a large box was laid over a steam vent. Inside, was a lump of blankets and boots, the shape of a man, knees bent.

"I don't see how you'd ever get over it."

He reached for my hand in the dark and held it a moment. "I don't want to get over it. I want to remember what happened every day of my life."

"I think I understand."

"My other daughter lives in New York with her husband. They have a four-year-old child. A beautiful little girl. Someday, I'd like you to meet them all."

I tripped over the sidewalk. It felt like a declaration of sorts. Meet my family. He grabbed my elbow to steady me, and we turned onto 102nd and came back and stood in front of number 217. Ichiro bent down and picked up Don Quixote. "Please take him," he said.

"I can't."

"Why not?"

"I don't know," I said. "I have nothing to give you." My teeth were chattering.

"Do you really mean that?"

"No, I suppose I don't." I took the knight errant. "Why don't you bring your violin over tomorrow night, and I'll accompany you on the Mendelssohn? I'd love to play it with you."

He made an O with his mouth, but no sound came out.

"Around eight?"

"I'm not up to snuff."

"At eight?"

18

I put Eemo to bed early, just before he knocked on the door. He'd spiffed himself up: shaved, put on a clean shirt, and combed his hair. In one hand, he held his violin case and music. In the other, a bunch of yellow lilies.

"I'm very nervous," he said, taking off his shoes at the door and giving me the flowers. We went into the kitchen, and I put the lilies in a vase, ran water into it, and set them on the kitchen counter.

I thanked him. "I never buy flowers for myself."

"How come?"

"I just don't. Do you?"

"No." He laughed. "Once I knew a woman who lived near a cemetery. She used to bring me bouquets after the mourners left. She only did it in the winter—to save the flowers, she said."

"Very bad karma. Someone you were with?"

"Not for long. Her name was Cynthia." He smiled. "Shall we?" He set the violin case on the floor and took out his instrument. He tightened the bow, rubbed rosin over the horsehair, and placed a folded handkerchief over the chin rest. I hit an *A*, and he began to tune. Violins, when they're tuned, always sound comical to me—maybe because

I grew up with a cello. But I didn't feel close to laughing. His hands trembled. They were very white and smooth. Scritch, scritch went the peg of the E-string.

"Another *A*," he said. At last, the string came into tune and held.

"Give me an idea of the tempo you'd like," I said.

"My goal is to get through the first half of the first page," he said. "That's all."

I started, and he followed on a high *B*. He made it through the first run, like a rider in a steeplechase, and through the second, but the horse threw him at the octave double stops.

"Those are murder," I said. I thought he might skip them and go on to an easier section.

"From the top again," he said. I glanced over at him. He was totally focused. Not nearly as mild a man as I'd thought. He played the double stops and kept going. I was right beside him then. Half a page later, he blundered through a passage and stopped. He tightened his bow, and we plunged back in, back through the double stops and on, through a few more pages.

"Okay," he said finally, "that's as far as I go in this movement. Do you want to try the *Andante*? I usually take it about like this." He sang the first few measures, one of my favorite of Mendelssohn's melodies, the long *E* followed by the downward triad from the *F*, and a leap to the high *A*. Ichiro's forehead knotted with concentration; he looked as though he might cry. I was bowled over by his playing.

"That was gorgeous," I said when we'd finished.

"Did you think so?"

"You have real feeling for it. And you haven't even raised a sweat."

"I don't sweat much. But dangerous overheating inside."

He lifted his violin. "Want to try again?"

How can I explain the effect of his playing on me? It took me back to my first serious music lessons. I climbed the stairs to the third floor of an old wooden building where there were two pianos and a view across rooftops. I always felt nervous mounting those stairs, almost physically sick at times. It was partly that I was never well enough prepared. But mostly, it was the brooding eyes of Gurevicius and what I knew he wanted to call from my heart. One day I was playing a Bach partita when he told me to stop. He sat down at the second piano. "Just listen." Huge chords rolled from him. He made an arc with his hand as it left the keyboard and came down again. His head was high, his eyes closed. The music poured out. Moussorgsky's *The Great Gate of Kiev*. When he finished, he said, *Play Bach as though you mean it, Nadia.*

As though you mean it. Ichiro played like that. Like the line in Casablanca. *Kiss me. Kiss me as if it were the last time.*

"Can we take it from measure 56?" he said. "One last time." I raised my chin, and he began. When we finished, I smiled at him. "You remind me of why I went into music in the first place."

"Do you mean that?"

"I try not to say things I don't mean." He bent to put his violin and bow back in the case and stood up.

When I try to remember how it happened, I'm blank. I might have tried to pass him, thinking to offer him something to drink. But when I came close, he took me by the shoulders and kissed me on the mouth. Quick and hard, like an exclamation point. And then again, more softly, parting my lips with his.

I was so astonished, I laughed.

"Forgive me," he said.

"There's nothing to forgive," I told him. I wish now I'd taken his hand and led him to the bedroom.

At this distance, I see I've spent most of a life walling myself off, trying to bring my body temperature down to something under the heat of blood because I'm scared of the world, its tempests of love, scared of the terriblenesses that fall out of the newspaper each day, scared that I'll hurt someone. My experience says that's what people do.

Ichiro picked up his violin case as though to leave.

"Don't go," I said. "You want a glass of wine? A cup of tea?"

"Tea would hit the spot."

We went into the kitchen, and I put the water on to boil.

"Where's Eemo?" he asked.

"In the bedroom. I put him to bed before you came." I looked at him and smiled. "I didn't expect you'd play the way you do."

"You thought I'd play like a man who mends fussy frames."

"I wouldn't put it like that."

"I'm sorry, Nadia."

"Please."

"I don't believe in just taking what I want."

"Please don't worry." The groove between his nose and lips shone with perspiration. I suddenly thought how handsome he was. I thought of laying my finger on that groove and saying, *Shhhhh.* I could have kissed him lightly on the cheek. I could have done many things, but I was off balance, clumsy. I brought the teapot and cups into the living room and asked him to move the piano bench close to the chairs. I set the tray down. I kicked off my shoes, slid them under the piano bench, and poured two cups of tea.

"It's rooibas, from South Africa."

"The tea?"

"Yes."

"Ah."

I sat down next to him, and we looked out the window at the sky. "Once," I told him, "I had a piano teacher named Antonin Gurevicius. He was Lithuanian. I don't know what he was doing in Nebraska. He was the best teacher I ever had. I wouldn't be a musician if it weren't for him. After I'd been his student for a while, he began to kiss me at the end of my lessons. They were serious kisses, grownup kisses. I was in my teens. It confused me. But I don't think there was anything wrong with what he did. I'm a better pianist because of it. Probably a better person."

"Your playing must have inflamed him," Ichiro murmured.

"It wasn't my playing, it was me."

He was quiet a moment and said, "I don't think it was wrong either. Perhaps he loved you a little."

19

On small screens all over the cabin, the movie is ending. A woman stands on a dock, waving to a man motoring away on a boat. It's twilight, and she turns slowly and walks away from the water toward her car. I don't have earphones, but I don't need them. The only surprising thing is that she doesn't throw herself into the water and swim toward the boat.

I don't believe in unadulterated happy endings. There's happiness, but not happiness without suffering. Not unless you're an enlightened being. But if you're enlightened, it seems as though you're inevitably alone. Ghandi. Mother Theresa. Mohammed. God.

Someone once said that a kiss is when two people get so close, they can't see anything wrong with each other. *Kiss me as if it were the last time.* I was completely surprised that night. I thought Ichiro had dispensed with love: too painful, his peace of mind too hard-earned.

Eemo had no such conflicts. He fell in love with a white pigeon this spring. "*Carroooo,*" she called from the ledge outside the window.

"*Trrrrrr…*" Eemo answered, cocking his head.

"*Carroooo.*" The pigeon bobbed her head up and down.

Eemo bobbed his head back and whisked his beak back and forth over the perch. "Bird-o?" His eyes dilated. He pranced up and down. He extended one leg and looked backwards over his shoulder, like Fred Astaire. He lowered his eyelids and stood there motionless, perfectly quiet. The pigeon dragged one wing along the ledge.

"*Trrrrr*," said Eemo again.

I tiptoed out and left them alone.

When I came back, the sun had gone down, and the pigeon was gone. Eemo appeared to be nest-building. He shredded a newspaper and stuffed it under the radiator. "Mr. Rogers haha?" He jammed another wad underneath.

In the kitchen, I poured myself a glass of wine, finished it off, and went back to check on him. When I got closer, he lunged at my feet.

"Bad bird!"

Later, I found him hunkered down, the feathers around his ruff raised, looking out from his nest. Exhausted, he hopped onto the dowel I stretched in front of him. I raised it to the cage, and he climbed onto his perch and locked his toes around the wood. His head sank into the feathers of his neck, and his eyes closed. I shut the door and covered the cage with the night curtain.

The white pigeon kept coming back. They spent their days together on opposite sides of the screen while I practiced for the Brahms concert. My father no longer answered the phone, but I called every day.

"He's been looking at the ceiling," Tricia said. "He was reaching for something with his hands. I asked him what he was doing. 'The field is ready for plowing,' he told me. He said something about a horse."

"Maybe I better come."

"When were you planning on?"

"The Monday after this one." I didn't know what to do. If I waited until after the Brahms, I'd have a whole week. If I went right away, I had to come straight back or find a substitute for the concert.

"I don't know. He goes up and down."

"You'll call if things change?"

"Of course. I'll see if I can put him on."

After a few minutes, I heard his voice on the other end, but not the words.

"I can't hear you," I said.

"I said it's going to be night here soon."

"Four-thirty your time, right?"

He didn't say anything.

"So how are you?"

He worked for air. "Your mother and I are going to the lake."

"The lake?"

He sounded annoyed. "Lake Nidzkie." He took a ragged breath.

He was talking about a lake in the northeast of Poland where we'd been once or twice before the war. I told him I could picture the island that disappeared in the rain.

"When we get there—" Another breath. "I'll show you how it works." There was a long pause. "Your mother told me what happened," he said. "I'm sorry."

I didn't know what he was talking about. "Never mind, *Tatuś*, it's all right now. Don't worry."

"After I'm gone," he said, "I'll see you in the air."

I began to cry on my end of the line, softly, so he couldn't hear.

"Don't cry," he said.

"I'll be there in about ten days," I said, "right after the concert. I'll come sooner if you want me to."

"No." He was emphatic.

"You know I love you," I said.

"You too. Now go make yourself some supper. I bet you haven't eaten." He labored for breath while I waited.

"Go on," he said.

He died that night in his sleep.

The phone rang before first light, rang and rang. And then I was scared, running toward it.

"Nadia?" Trish said, "He's gone, honey." She began to cry. "I was sleeping in the chair next to his bed. I got up and put my hand on his chest and couldn't feel his heartbeat."

At first, I felt nothing. I said what needed to be said. "I'll be there as soon as I can. I think there needs to be a death certificate. Could you call his doctor? And then please leave him as he is? I'll call again and let you know when I'm coming."

I went to the kitchen and scrambled an egg and left it in a bowl. It was five-thirty in the morning. I turned in circles, went out in the hall and knocked softly on Ichiro's door. There was no sound. I waited until six and called him on the phone.

"I have to ask you to take Eemo again," I said. "I have to go to Nebraska as soon as I can."

"Hold on," he said, "I'll be right there."

He came to the door in a bathrobe, and it hit me then: my father was gone.

Ichiro held me while I sobbed.

Finally, he said, "He died in his sleep?"

"Yes. Trish was asleep in a chair beside him."

"He wasn't in pain?"

"I don't know."

"…Listen, I can help you find a flight."

"I should have been with him."

He took me by the shoulders and said I was the best daughter anyone could have.

Three hours later, I was on a plane, looking down at Pennsylvania fields. All at once, I could see my father's life, whole, like a landscape from above. How huge it was—all he'd seen and lived and been. And how tiny in the face of the stars.

Trish was asleep on the couch when I walked in the door of my father's house. She opened her eyes and told me she felt closer to my father than she ever had to her own. It gave me an odd feeling, as though my father had picked up another daughter in the last few weeks. I tucked the blankets around her and went to his bedroom.

Whatever had inhabited him was gone. I thought I wouldn't know what to do. But I still loved what was left, that earthly husk. His mouth had fallen open. He seemed to be saying, *Let me speak.* I touched one of his eyebrows, and then the other, smoothing them, but they refused smoothing. His face looked unconcerned, at ease, like the boy in the rowboat.

I went into the bathroom and came back with a clean washcloth and a pan of warm water. I set the pan on a stool and dipped the washcloth in and wrung it out. Under his eye, a tear had dried white. I washed it off and ran the washcloth over his forehead and eyelids and nose. I dipped again and washed his ears and hands. Over the years his nails had developed permanent ridges, like raked earth. His fingers no longer straightened out completely. I thought of washing all of him, but I imagined his voice, *Why bother?* I squeezed lotion into my hand and rubbed it onto his face, over his forehead and the bridge of his nose, over the top of his cheek. I kissed him and cried a little more, thinking he wouldn't want me to be making all this fuss. I pulled the covers up over his shoulders and tucked him in.

Halfway down the hall, I realized I'd never again hear his voice say *Nadia*, or hear him call me his little cabbage. It was as though my name had dropped off the face of the earth. I slid down the wall and cried on the floor, sounds coming from me I didn't know what to do with. I went back and kissed him once more and sat beside him until I was able to leave.

That night, I dreamt that he and I were in a boat together. The sky was thick with clouds. Every so often, a ray of sun shot through, making a trail of brightness all the way down to earth. My father rowed toward a reedy spot at the end of the lake. "We're almost there," he said. A swan was sitting on its haunches on the far bank like a savage, its white face shining through reeds.

"Rock!" I shouted, but my father kept straining at the oars, oblivious. We struck hard and capsized in deep water and then we were in a great hall, my great-grandfather seated in the center of a circle of relations. With him were Grandmother Helene, Uncle Janek, great Aunt Lydia Bartoszewski and her son Jakub, Uncle Ludwik and Aunt Angela, all of them dead in the war.

Three days later, we held the service on the covered terrace that looked out onto the chicken enclosure. Charlie, my father's best friend, was there. Freddy Bernicki, an old friend who'd served in the army with my father, arrived from Omaha. A man from the hardware store came from town, along with Olly, the chicken man, and the family up the road.

The service was short. Freddy Bernicki told a story about my father falling into a latrine in Italy during the war. Charlie spoke and broke down in the middle of it, took a minute to compose himself, and went on to say Mike Korczak was the best friend he ever had.

"Everywhere he went," I said, "he planted things. If he'd lived in the Sahara, he would have made things grow." I said some other things too, in both Polish and English. But what I remember is the spring thunder rumbling in the west, the rain letting loose.

Afterwards, our small group milled around the kitchen and living room. While I was getting the sandwiches out, Freddy told me how my father had helped his son after he got out of prison. "He gave him a couple hundred bucks to buy a car. Did he ever tell you that?"

"No. What's your son doing now?"

"He's a welder over in Kearney. His wife's a kindergarten teacher."

Trish set out drinks and glasses. Charlie had brought beer and a couple bottles of vodka; by mid-afternoon, everyone was half-drunk, with the exception of the neighbor kids. Freddy finally headed back to Omaha, and Charlie gave me an awkward, lurching hug. "I'll miss him, the old devil." He pressed a photograph of my father and him into my hand and stumbled out the door. I imagined him sitting in his car and crying for a bit before starting down the road.

Then the neighbors left, and Olly and I went out to the chickens. "Are you okay with taking them?" I asked. "You might want to think about it. This probably sounds crazy, but he wanted them to die natural deaths. I think he had a little graveyard back there."

"I'll be damned." Olly's nose looked as though it had been broken once or twice. His face was a quilt of pits and wrinkles. "I don't mind letting them die naturally, but one thing I don't do is chicken funerals, all due respect."

I laughed. "No funerals."

"Don't you worry, honey, I'll treat them like royalty."

"He left plenty to cover their feed," I said. "Do you want to take the whole shebang?"

"What? The coop? What do you want for it?"

"For heaven's sakes."

Tricia was the last to leave. It turned out her car had died for good the day before, and she needed a ride. "Isn't that weird?" she said. "Right when your father died. It was like it knew."

"Why don't you take his car," I said.

"If you don't mind. I'll get someone to bring me back tomorrow."

"I mean, take it. I'll have to find the title. It needs tires, but it runs. It'll save me having to sell it."

"I'm not allowed to take gifts in my work."

"You're not working for us anymore. You stopped yesterday." I went digging in a drawer and found the title, forged my father's signature, and signed it over to her. As the Oldsheimer went down the road, it jerked a little as though it was coughing. A puff of gray smoke shot out of the exhaust pipe, and then it was on its way.

The thunder rumbled to itself as the storm headed west. *After I'm gone*, I heard my father say, *I'll see you in the air.*

20

When I got back to New York, Ichiro brought me take-out from a Thai restaurant. He came to the door and put the paper bag in my hands and left quickly so I wouldn't need to make conversation if I didn't want to. I ate a little and played Chopin's Nocturne in E-minor. It wasn't long before Eemo was wailing, "Oh, weyy, Oh weyyy!" as though his heart was breaking.

The next day Peter came over, shuffling, a little embarrassed, with a book of Rilke poetry.

Later, Margot took me out to lunch. I told her how my father had planted tulips outside our rented house. I told her about the seizures he suffered after the war. A door would bang somewhere in the house, and he'd look as though he'd been shot, his eyes frozen wide open. My mother would lead him, stiff-legged, to the couch and lay him down and cover him with a blanket. It went on for a few years, and finally it stopped.

I didn't worry about blabbing at Margot, we've known each other so long, but there was so much to say, impossible to turn it all over, like a huge field that needed tilling. What to do with it all? What to do with my father, my mother, my grandmother, Reba, Władysław, all of them as alive in me today as they ever were? What to do with all the people we left behind, a morning on the hill above the river, the creak of a floorboard in a house that's probably no longer standing?

My father died over and over in my head. I kept imagining the moment he stopped breathing, the violent stillness. I remember the day we drove to the doctor's office in Lincoln, the wind blowing the car sideways as we drove back home.

I asked myself why I hadn't stopped working for a couple of months. I could have cooked food for him those last weeks, taken him for drives. It's fashionable now for the living to tell the dying, "It's all right, you can go now," as though it has anything to do with us. Without being conscious of it, I expected to say something of the sort to my father. It seems silly now. It still surprises me how little his death had to do with me, how alone we all are at the end.

Every day, I walked to the park to visit that old beech tree. It was beginning to green out on a few of its upper branches, and I found comfort standing near its trunk.

One April day, an odd misty rain fell, tiny droplets settling on the skin. Everything felt new-begotten, hopeful even. I swung my arms and felt a small stab of joy, the first since my father's death. But no sooner had I noticed it than it was gone. *Come back, Tatuś,* I said. *You've been gone long enough now. What made you think you could just walk off the edge of the world without saying goodbye?* The rain collected on my arms, and I wiped it off with my fingers.

Down the stone steps, I walked into the lower part of the park. Two trucks were parked at a distance from the old tree. I heard the noise of a chain saw but thought nothing of it. I'd expected the park people any day to come trim out the old wood and shore the beech up for another season. But when I looked into the sky, the tree wasn't there.

Everything went red. I began to run. My hair spilled out from under my hat, my shoes sucked mud, the men stood over the trunk with chain saws, a carpet of sawdust under their boots. I grabbed a man's sleeve and yanked the saw from him. I felt arms around me. Shouts. I was thrown to the ground.

By the time I was brought into the emergency room, my hat was gone. My clothes were covered with mud. "I don't want it, I don't want it!" I cried when they tried to give me a sedative. "I'll stop, I promise!" I dug in my purse for my wallet and managed to bring out one of my cards: Anna Korczak, Professional Musician.

For some reason, they let me be. I don't know how long I was there. People came and went. A teenage boy in the next cubicle had to have glass dug out of his foot. An old woman on the other side coughed like she was bringing up asphalt.

After a time, a nurse came into the cubicle to say they'd release me into someone's care if I thought I could manage. She gave me a piece of paper with the name of several counselors and psychiatrists and a handout about staying away from alcohol and drugs. She said there was a man in the waiting room who'd agreed to take me home.

"What man?"

"From the city park crew."

"All right," I said, and she led me out to the waiting room by one elbow as though I were flammable. The city employee turned out to be a middle-aged black guy with a pocked face. His hair was beginning to gray, and sawdust stuck to his forehead.

"You feeling better?" he asked. "I told the crew I'd see you home."

In the cab, he said in a stern voice, "You know, that saw was still running when you grabbed at it. It took three of us to get you to the ground."

"My father just died. I visited that tree every day."

He was quiet a minute. "You know, honey, it had to come down."

"I'm not blaming you."

"I understand."

His hand was warm when he took mine. "You got anyone at home to look after you?" he asked.

"Yes." I didn't want him worrying.

I paid the driver, and Samuel made sure I got upstairs. I never thanked him properly. I don't know his last name. He just said, "You take care of yourself now, you hear?"

"Oh, weyy!" cried Eemo when he heard me crying. He pulled himself up one side of his cage, over the top, and down the other side.

I got in the shower, and the water ran down the drain, mud-colored. My hair was filthy, tangled with wood shavings. I slept fourteen hours that night. I don't remember getting into bed.

Last year at the Metropolitan, I saw a Rembrandt self-portrait, painted in his last decade of life. Under his eyes were large violet pouches. His forehead was deeply folded—rucked and creased like a river. I remember the wreckage of Rembrandt's skin, the eyes that looked both into this world and the next. There was weariness in them, mixed with humility. All men must die, they said.

21

The priest has gone to the bathroom. Across the aisle, the baby fusses. I smile at her mother, who looks exhausted. "Want me to hold her for a minute?" I ask in Polish. She passes the baby across, and I take her onto my lap and bounce her up and down. She looks uncertain and then laughs. The mother watches. She tells me that she's going to Limanowa to see her sister who's also just had a baby.

Later this spring, the white pigeon came back to the windowsill with a dusky gray boyfriend. Eemo didn't seem to worry about the boyfriend. He made soft noises to himself, flew into the bedroom, picked out a bit of hair from my brush and stuffed it into his nest, under the radiator. While I ate breakfast, he preened, pulled his flight feathers through his beak, smoothed and oiled them.

One day, Maria called and said that Linda Kopecky had let her know that the Jacob Horowitz in Łódź had a wife and five children. "He told the Red Cross person a lie. He say he is born in Rzezów, and he knows no one named Maria Horowitz. The Jacob I know is not born in Rzezów, but his grandfather is born there. So what I think, he is telling me to leave him alone."

"What are you going to do?"

"Forget about him."

"Can you do that?"

"Yes."

We were quiet a moment. I told her I was sorry.

"Me also…Too many years, you know?"

"He must have thought you didn't make it through the war."

There was silence. And then with passion, she said, "If you see that Jacob Horowitz in Łódź…if you see him, tell him Maria waited all these years."

"I'll do that."

"Łódź is terrible place."

"I've never been there."

"Terrible place. Don't go there."

"Are you okay?"

"Pootsie is here."

"How is he?"

"Doing fine."

"I got a plane ticket yesterday," I told her. "I don't know whether I'll see you before I go. But soon after I get back. You want me to bring you anything?"

"No, no, you come over when you come back. I cook for you. You have a good trip, Nadia. If you have boyfriend, I cook for him too. Now we both can have boyfriend. But first I tell priest to make me unmarried."

I laughed. "We'll go to a single's club," I said. Within a year, I thought, she'd be dead. But no, I don't really believe that.

I put on a long-sleeved shirt and went outdoors. It was one of those first heartbreakingly beautiful spring days, the sky newly washed, a renaissance of small green leaves. People wore shorts, daffodils bloomed under trees. A young guy walked along the sidewalk, came to a fire hydrant and hopped to the top with one foot, did a 360 degree twirl, and kept going.

My father was dead. How could there be all this life?

On Broadway, a man stood in front of a portable punching bag. He struck it over and over while sweat flew from him. The sound was rhythmic—*whappety boom, whappety boom*—like a kind of music.

I walked up Amsterdam to 106th and east toward Central Park. Inside the gates, I sat down on a bench and leaned into the sun. Nearby, a theological argument was going on. A young black guy in combat boots and camouflage pants was talking to another young guy and an older man. "

When it says God created man from dirt, it don't mean *dirt!*" He leaned over and picked up a handful. "Not dirt. He meant sperm. God created man from *sperm*. How come Adam and Eve fucked? They fucked because God fucked. You have to listen to the words, brother, not just the words, but what's underneath. Like with Moses. Moses ain't never parted no water. Ain't no man never parted water. That was *never* the case. He parted water as in wisdom. What they're talking about is wisdom."

He sat down on a bench. The second guy said, "The Bible is shit, man."

"Don't call the Bible shit," the older man said.

"Hey, man, what you talking about? God didn't write the Bible. It was written by umpty-ump people. You think God wrote the Bible, you full of shit."

"Why you suppose Jesus created white and black?" said the first man. "Why didn't he make them all the same color?"

"Jesus was black, " said the second man. "He was living in Egypt. *Think* about it, it's common sense. White people can't survive that kind of heat. So he *had* to be black. Why'd

He make whitey?...Why'd he make flies? He made nuisances to deepen the souls of black folk. To deepen them."

I walked back, and the pugilist was still punching, no faster, no slower than he'd been an hour ago. His eyes looked dazed, a man reduced to fists. At his feet, there were a few dollars in a donation box.

We played Brahms on a Sunday to an overflow audience, the music carrying us, lifting off. I wasn't nervous for once. The *Rondo alla Zingarese* is a lulu, loaded with syncopation and a tricky set of runs that need to be solid, light, bell-like. Everything dropped away—the audience with its coughs and shiftings, the room, the glare of lights—leaving only the music. It was like coming into a clearing that's never known the gabble and frantic rushings and anxieties of the world. I love playing with this group.

After the concert, the cellist asked how I was doing. He was a sweaty bear, his face overheated from the last movement. "I lost my own father two years ago," he said. "He was in Denmark—I never got a chance to say goodbye. My mother's sick now."

"Will you go over?"

"Not until summer."

"I'm going back to Poland soon. I wish I'd gone with my father."

"Maybe he couldn't bring himself to go." He gestured toward the reception area where people milled around. "I guess we better go do our social duty."

"I can't handle it, Franz, I'm sorry." I kissed him goodbye, skirted the crowd, and waved goodbye to the violist and violinist.

A warm wind blew, people on the street looked as though

a weight had been lifted. For the first time since my father's death, life felt possible. The concert went better than I'd expected. The rondo was a romp. Actually more like a rout, we took it so fast.

In Chinatown, all the Canal Street jewelry stores sparkled. The stores were empty, but they filled me with hopefulness—engagement rings by the handful, the sparkly little pendants for girls' necks, diamond earrings for a true love.

I was wearing a long, sleeveless dress in a clingy grayish-purple silk, with a light shawl over the top. I stopped in at a little hole-in-the-wall restaurant for dim sum and sat at a formica table. A waiter brought me a bamboo container of dumplings. I ate quickly, dipping them in sauce with chopsticks, emptied out and happy.

When I came back out onto the street, the wind had picked up; it looked like rain. I pulled the shawl around me. But something else was happening, some kind of disturbance. A chicken had gotten loose and was running down the sidewalk, this way and that. No one seemed to know what to do. A few people stopped and watched; many kept going, as though there was no chicken at all. In its panic, it flew out into the street, and a huge produce truck ran right over the top of it. I put my hand over my mouth. After the truck went on, the chicken lay on the pavement. I stepped into the street, whipped off my shawl, and gathered it up the way I've seen Polish peasants do a hundred times.

It wasn't dead. The beak was parted, and it panted quickly. Holding it in my arms, I covered its head with my shawl, thinking to give it darkness and let it die in peace.

"Could you get me a cab?" I asked an older Chinese man standing next to me.

"Don't speak English." He backed away.

A woman tried for one, and the second cab stopped.

She opened the door and shut it behind me.

"217 West 102nd Street," I said to the driver. "Between Broadway and Amsterdam."

"What do you have there?" he asked.

"A chicken. It was running down the sidewalk, and then it went out in the street and a truck ran over it."

"You're kidding, right?"

"No."

"You sure it's not a dead chicken?"

"I don't think so."

"What are you going to do with it?"

"I don't know."

He laughed all the way to 102nd. When he stopped, I held out a twenty. "No, no," he said. "You made my day." I sat in the back of the cab with the chicken in my arms, shocked.

"Please," I said.

"No, no. If it lives, call her Elsie. After my wife." He got out his side and opened the door for me. "She won't believe this."

"You sure?"

"I already told you, now get outta here."

I couldn't get over it. I walked up the steps and shifted the chicken over to my right side. I managed to open the first door, then the second, and started up the stairs. The locks to my apartment need two hands, and I had to do a crouch, balancing the chicken with my forearms.

"Mr. Rogers, haha?" said Eemo.

"It's not funny," I said, heading toward the bedroom.

With one foot, I tipped over a cardboard box filled with clean clothes, dragged the box across the room with my toe to dislodge the laundry, and turned it right side up. I loosened the shawl and let it fall into the bottom of the box.

Gently, I laid the chicken inside. She was still alive but lay on one side, her eyes half closed. She was dirty from the street, bleeding near one wing, and some of her feathers were missing. Birds die quickly when they go into shock. I learned that from my father. I closed the cardboard flaps and went into the kitchen for a glass of water and an eye dropper. I came back to the bedroom, opened the box, held the chicken's head, and put a little water in the corner of her beak. She thrashed and went still. I gave her a small amount again, and this time, she swallowed. I closed the flaps of the box and left the room.

When I came back half an hour later, she was standing up. Good god! I went into the kitchen for more water while Eemo snuck into the bedroom. When I came back, there he was, flying at Elsie's eyes.

"Bad, bad boy!" He lunged at me as I tried to pick him up. I grabbed hold and shut him in his cage.

"Rawckkk!" he screamed.

"Don't *ever* do that again! Do you hear me?"

"Oh, weyy! Oh weyyy!" His cries turned self-pitying.

"Shut up! She got run over."

"You going out?" Ichiro asked on the stairs. He held open a cloth bag with different colors of plastic coated wire. "Look what I found."

"What are you making?"

"I don't know yet."

"Here's a question for you," I said. "Did you happen to see a big box anywhere in your travels? I brought home a chicken."

"What do you want a box for?"

"She's alive."

"You've got a live chicken upstairs in your apartment."

"Yes."

"You're joking."

Why did everyone think I was joking? I started down the stairs.

"…I think I saw a playpen over on Columbus," he said. "I could check if it's still there."

"You have time for this?"

"What's the alternative?" He sounded impatient.

"Tell me where it is, I'll find it."

He turned and held both my hands. "I want to help you."

We headed downstairs.

"How'd the concert go?" he asked.

"I shouldn't have said don't come. It went great."

"Never mind."

"Are you always so understanding?"

"No, I'm *not*. I like having my own way. I'm over-attached to my little routines. I hate it when I'm interrupted, when plans change too quickly. Like now. But then I get over it."

"What is this, full disclosure?" I asked as we headed east. "Well, I'm not perfect either. I hate cooking. I have a mediocre credit rating. I stay up until two in the morning. I don't generally like movies. I have an irrational fear of drowning."

"I wouldn't have guessed that."

"What?"

"The fear of drowning."

"I had a sadistic swim instructor. I'll tell you about him some time."

"Did you read the news story a couple days ago about

the guy in Tokyo who was afraid of tidal waves? He invented a pair of inflatable underpants which accidentally blew up during rush hour."

"You made that up."

"I swear to god. He was reaching in his vest pocket for a piece of hard candy and hit the rip cord. Someone had to puncture them with a pencil."

We both started laughing and couldn't stop. And then we walked along in silence a few steps. I looked at him sideways. "You know, we've been calling each other friends for a while now."

"Aren't we?"

My stomach contracted with what I was about to say. "What I think is this. I think it's a naturally unstable situation for a man and woman to be friends, just friends. Unless one of them is gay or they're ninety years old…"

"What are you saying?"

"I don't know. What *are* we?"

"Friends."

"We've been playing it very safe."

"I don't want that forever," he said.

"You don't?"

"No."

"I don't know what I want. I don't want to hurt you."

"I have a suggestion," he said. "Why don't we just watch and see what happens?"

"And then what?"

"Then in a few months, we'll see where we are."

"And what if we're somewhere we don't want to be?"

"How would that happen?" he asked.

"Maybe it wouldn't…My mother used to say, 'Don't push the river, let it flow by itself.'"

My grandmother used to say, "*Sumeba miyako.*" Wherever you live, you come to love it."

"Then it doesn't matter where you are."

"Yes, it does. It matters quite a lot." He turned and kissed me. "You don't need to worry."

"And why is that?"

"It's out of our control, whatever it is." He smiled.

The playpen was under the tree where he remembered. "What do you think?" He looked at me as though we were picking out our first dining room set together.

"Do you think she'd be able to get out?"

"You could stretch netting across the top."

"It's good."

He picked it up.

"Did your mother ever put you in one of these?" I asked.

"I doubt it. I remember her wheeling my brothers around in a wheelbarrow. She didn't like that they couldn't see the sky from the baby carriage…She must have been disappointed none of her boys became artists."

"You did."

"Not really." He picked up a piece of one-by-four leaning against a tree to block a hole where one of the spindles had fallen out. "Anyone could do what I do. But I never knew anyone who'd pick up a live chicken off the street."

"Plenty of people."

"Who? You didn't see anyone else rushing for that chicken, did you?"

When we got back, Elsie was out of the box, scratching

around in the clean laundry. "She's bleeding," he said.

"If she hasn't died by now, she's going to recover."

"You think so?"

"I'm sure of it."

I was about to thank him for his help when he suddenly said, "Why don't I take her?"

"What are you talking about?"

"I've got less to worry about than you do."

"I brought her home, she's my problem."

"I'd *like* to keep her," he said.

"Because you feel sorry for me?"

"No."

"I think that's what it is. You don't think I can manage one more thing."

"There's nothing you can't manage."

"I was thinking I could rent a car and drive her out to Nebraska to be with my father's chickens," I said. "I've got to go back and settle the house anyway."

He looked at me. "That's not a practical idea. You don't want to drive all that way with a chicken. Why don't I just take her?"

We set up the playpen in the small room off his living room, and he hammered the one by four into place. I washed the whole thing down, covered the bottom with newspapers, brought some of Eemo's food and a dish of water, and set Elsie in. She scratched around and had a sip of water.

"She likes it," I said.

"You'll teach me about chickens?"

"There's nothing to learn. Food, water, a dry place to sleep, keep her away from coyotes."

22

Three more hours, and we'll be landing in Warsaw. It feels as though my soul is shifting back toward youth, toward a state of unfiltered openness, when happiness was complete in itself, and sadness and terror, when they came, were similarly single-minded—like a sky with one hue.

When I lived with my grandmother in Piaseczno, my companions were two boys, several years older. There were no girls in the village the same age or older, and only a few younger. I preferred the company of Stefan and Andrzej, when they'd have me. Stefan lived up the road from us; he was just fourteen when my mother and I left Piaseczno for the United States. Andrzej lived a short walk out of town. For a time, I didn't know which one of them I'd marry. Stefan, the more serious of the two and the one I knew first, spoke so shyly one day, I thought I'd misheard. *When the war's over, you'll want to go to university. I'll wait for you.*

But it didn't start out like that. It began with him calling me stupid because I couldn't name the smallest planet.

"*Nie, nie jestem!*"

"*Jesteś!*"

No I'm not, yes you are! I bit him on the hand. He wrestled me to the ground. He ripped my coat, and then we were friends. His right eye was a little bigger than the left, and his smile wider on the right than the left, as though he'd gotten tipped sideways when he was made. One day after school, he led me up a ladder to the loft above his barn. His mother kept geese, and their feathers blew around the floor below. We sat in the hay and talked about the movement of planets around the sun, the impossible heat and cold of those places. I asked him whether he'd rather live on Mars or Venus. "Mars, of course. If you're freezing, you can do something about it—build a fire, wrap yourself in quilts, but if your skin's on fire…"

Up in the loft, he circled my knee with the tip of his finger.

"…That tickles."

"Do you like it?"

"Yes." His fingernail was dirty and exciting.

"Can I kiss you?"

When I opened my eyes, it looked as though his eyes had multiplied. He turned his head to one side, his lips still on mine. He stopped. "Is it okay?"

"Yes." As a girl, I'd heard that the Black Madonna of Częstochowa wept real tears. I felt like crying, laughing all at once.

After that, we went up there every chance we got. Now I think I was too young for what we did. But the war speeded everything up. We made a nest in the hay with an old quilt. Off came his sweater and school shirt, frayed at the collar, his pants; off came my coat and sweater and blouse and skirt. Down to our underwear, we kissed and stroked each other until the trees grew dark outside and our mothers called to us. They must have known what was going on; but they had other things on their minds.

Every Saturday, Stefan bathed in an oval tub on the

floor next to his wood stove. I loved to think of him there. On top of the stove was one of his mother's cooking pots; next to him, a dented enamel pitcher sat on a rough shelf. I imagined him sliding down, his eyes closed, until warm water covered his chest and stomach.

My mother and I left for the border in the middle of the night; I was never able to say goodbye to Stefan or Andrzej. For years, I was mad at my mother for not letting me do that one thing. She said there was no time. If we missed the ride, we might never get another.

I see myself bumping along, in the back of the truck, against my will. A wool dress and thick stockings and leather boots that laced above my ankles. A young body swaddled in two sweaters, a cloth raincoat, too small, bunched around the sweaters and drawn over my knees. A shapeless black hat, round as a melon, with a white fringe decoration that had ripped off everywhere but over my left eyebrow. Light brownish hair spilling out from under it. Sunken cheeks. Dark eyebrows over dark eyes. A full mouth saying nothing. A chin holding itself too high. A scarf around the top of my coat, my hands loosening it to open my throat to the night, as though I had to feel this one thing, this cold on my throat. There was devastation wherever we looked, roofs fallen in, walls blackened by fire, pockmarked with bullets. Near the border, the sun rose and mists hung over the fields. It took us three more years to get out of Europe: Slovakia, France and finally, Sweden.

When at last we reached New York, we took a bus all the way west to Grand Island, through the bellies of the Allegheny Mountains, in and out of tunnels with strange names: Kittatinny, Tuscarora. Outside Erie, Pennsylvania, I remember an ugly strip-mined hill, two men riding bicycles silhouetted against the sky. Cleveland, Toledo, Chicago, and then into the flatlands of Iowa, so flat you wanted to scream.

I wrote to Stefan from Nebraska, but he never answered. Maybe because I left without saying goodbye. Or because my words didn't say what I felt. Or because he'd changed. I wrote him during those months when I had no words, when words were worthless rags. Gradually I lost his bright eyes, his voice. Most people get over this sort of thing. But tonight, I understand he's been with me these years like a phantom, a blueprint for how life might have been.

I'll meet Marek and his wife when I get to Warsaw, and their small daughters. Marek is my father's cousin's son. And from there, who knows? I lay my head back on the seat and fall asleep.

In a dream, a cup of coffee cools at my father's bedside. The windows have no glass; snow gathers on the windowsills and piles up on the floor. The only sign of life is the steam rising from my father's cup. And then that disappears until there's just snow falling.

When I wake, landing time is twenty minutes away. I feel scared. Below, the fields are small patches of color. A sparkle of dew catches the sun next to a square house in the middle of an empty field.

"How did you sleep?" the priest asks.

"Pretty well, and you?"

"Like a broken drum. Ha ha. Couldn't be beat." He must have picked that up in Missouri. "Will you stay in Warsaw tonight?" he wants to know.

"For three or four nights." The plane is low now, on the

outskirts of the city. I can make out a person walking along a dirt path. And then we're over the airport. Brown dirt, brown sky, brown everything, a few ugly buildings. When the plane hits the runway, there's a sound like gravel thrown against the windows—passengers are clapping their hands in gratefulness. I touch the box that holds my father's ashes. *We made it, Tatuś!*

The airplane's a hubbub of Polish, and then a free-for-all as people grab bags and head for the exit. The priest turns and wishes me a good visit. The baby across the aisle is crying. The man with the big head holds the elbow of the black-haired woman, as though he's blind. I catch a glimpse of the black guy who'll be making a film.

Let me off! Let me off!

As my feet touch the ground outside the airport, a lump catches in my throat. But there's no time to think. People are knocking into each other, hollering. The air is murky, like industrial sludge. A taxi driver tries to cheat me first thing. "Two-hundred thousand zlotys to the city, special for you, madam." he says.

"*Ty jesteś złodziej!*" I cry. You're a thief! Fifty-thousand zlotys, Marek said it should cost. I board a bus, and it roars out of the airport with half its exhaust system missing. Two teenage girls in front of me talk loudly and kiss each other on the lips. I don't know, do kids generally do that here? Across the aisle, a woman says, "*Tak tak tak tak.*" I'd forgotten that rapid fire *yes, yes, yes.*

Out the window, a few feet underneath the cement streets, lies the rubble of old Warsaw: rotted lace curtains and leather corsets, canary cages and cooking pots, carousel horses, opera glasses, umbrellas, woolen hats. The bones of

Uncle Jan, my father's brother, and his wife and three children.

My father never told me that Marek and Olesia's daughter had Down's syndrome. Maybe he didn't know. Marta has straw-colored hair, a beautiful smile and eyes the color of shale. "I'm sorry," Marek says, "that we haven't got enough room for you to stay with us. If things were different, Olesia would be able to work, but as it is—" He gestures to the two small rooms. Olesia pours coffee while Marta toddles over and pats me on the leg. Her face is flat, her nose and ears undersized. Her tongue works outside her mouth.

The baby wakes, Olesia goes to her, and I nearly cry out when I see her face. Her muscles are slack like her sister's, with the same small nose and ears as Marta's.

Marek suggests we walk over to their friend Martin's apartment where I'm to stay. I hang onto the bag with my father's ashes in it; Marek carries the suitcase. We go several blocks and come to a concrete apartment building, maybe fifteen stories high. The elevator is blocked with a slab of plywood. As we climb the concrete stairs to the tenth floor, Marek tell me that hundreds of these buildings went up during the occupation.

The apartment overlooks the highway and is sparsely furnished with pseudo-Danish modern. I'm so tired I trip over the floor. We go back down the stairs and stop at the grocery store. A few grandmothers in babushkas are shopping there, but mostly, thin, high-wired women rush down the narrow aisles. All the jars and packages look strange. Turnips, cabbages, knobby carrots, unrecognizable lumps wrapped in cellophane. Marek buys beer, and on the way back, he tells me about his work at a hospital as a maintenance man for pulmonary and cardiac machines. An unassuming kindness clings to him like a good smell. He's a handsome man—his face narrowing at the chin, thin straight lips.

At five, Olesia sets dinner on the table, a cheese pudding with mushrooms, fried potatoes, a dish of beets. A store-bought cake. Beer. Vodka. She's a beauty: large eyes and hair the same color as Marta's.

Marek asks about my father, what he looked like, how he made a living. He tells me that his father was a farmer who died of emphysema.

"They were first cousins," I say. "What does that make us?"

"*Nie wiem*," he says. I don't know. "Some kind of cousins." Olesia dishes out the cheese pudding and fried potatoes. Marek's grandfather and mine—the oldest and middle brother of the family—had a falling out over a woman. The brothers never spoke to each other, although they lived in the same town.

Olesia slides the dish of beets toward me.

"Everything's delicious."

"I cook like peasant," she says. "Not fancy...Did you know when Marek's grandfather died, your grandfather married his widow?"

"I remember my father saying something about it."

"Your grandfather was waiting all his life. But he lived only a month after that."

"Getting his heart's desire must have been too big of a shock."

"At least he could die in peace," said Olesia.

"Or maybe he found she wasn't worth waiting for," Marek said.

"Wah!" Olesia said, "What a thing to say. Where's your romance?"

"What do you mean? I waited two years for you."

"But a lifetime?" she insisted.

"A lifetime is a long time," said Marek.

"I'd be worth it," she said, grabbing up a daughter in each arm to get them ready for bed.

Marek brings out the last letter my father sent them, dated Christmas, 1994, and lays it in my lap. My father's note talked about the tornadoes that blew through Grand Island that summer. He mentioned my visit coming up in January. It's odd to see his crabbèd hand, the words written in red ink: *She'll be able to spend a week with me. So far, not much snow, but it's coming.* He'll never anticipate my coming again; the house is emptied of all reason for visiting.

Suddenly I'm exhausted and can hardly sit upright. I'm too out of it to care, but Olesia sees when she comes out of the bedroom. "Marek, you must walk Nadia."

I wake in the dark, toward morning, on top of the covers. At first I can't remember where I am. In a dream, I've been playing my grandmother's piano. The piano room, with its brown-striped wallpaper and the faded pink roses, is gradually filling with water. The piano stool is polished wood, dark on the outside of the circle, lighter at the center. When I put my palm on the wooden seat and spin it around, the stool wobbles across the floor on iron legs and the water turns back, as though the piano stool is a spigot. My mother is there, opening her cello case with the sea green velvet lining.

She and I used to play cello-piano duets. Simple things.

I'd wait for her to lift the instrument out. I felt grown up sitting on the piano bench, listening to her tune, as though we were equals.

The day my father left for the war, the air was disturbed by wind and crows. His uniform smelled like dust. After he was gone, my mother stared out the window. I watched to see where her eyes went. She was looking for him. The next spring, purple violets came up under the window. Still, he didn't come. He didn't come and didn't come, until not coming was who he was.

Olesia and I visit St. Anne's church and Pilsudski Square with the children. A park near the tomb of the unknown soldier has open grass and trees where parents come with their kids. The second day we're together, Olesia asks me to keep an eye on Marta and the baby while she runs across the street to the bank. She takes off across the grass like a girl. The baby goes to sleep. I sit on the ground while Marta touches my face. Pat, pat. Her hands are like dry leaves. In a jerky, hallowed fashion, a big, smiling, spacious love pours from her. In any school, she'd be called slow. But that's because schools only think about brains.

Olesia comes back, out of breath. "The line at the bank was too long." Marta holds out her hands, and Olesia grabs her up.

On my own, I walk the city—up and down Jerozolimskie Avenue and through the Praga District and down Marsza-kowska Street—but I can't find the old Warsaw anywhere. In the beginning of the war, 60,000 people died here. Rubble from palaces, theaters, the opera house, homes, government buildings, parks, cafés burned red against the sky. Five years later, 200,000 people lost their lives in Warsaw during the fifty-six days of the Uprising. It must have been hell on earth. Bodies of patients and nurses hung from the windows at the hospital, buildings were burned one by one, until Warsaw vanished.

I picture the wide avenues, once here, the graceful buildings and large trees, people walking arm in arm, women with big bosoms, my father next to me, holding my hand. A horse-drawn *dorożka* pulled a carriage. My father asked if I'd like to go on a carousel, and I said yes although I had no idea what a carousel was; I heard music in the distance, and through the trees, something moving. A dark, greasy man took my ticket, and my father lifted me onto the back of a black horse. I put my arms around its painted neck while my father stood under a linden tree, waving.

Now, industrial air clogs my lungs. In the old market square stand replicas of ruined buildings, built brick by brick after the war, to look exactly like the buildings destroyed. It's like a hallucination. History has been erased.

In a book of photographs I once saw about the Warsaw Uprising, a child on a street holds a small dog, buildings smolder, ruins stand black against the sky. A woman lies on the pavement, wounded. A small boy stands over her.

23

Marek offers to drive me to Bieńkówka, and I ask him why we don't all go.

"No, no," says Olesia, "you and Marek go."

"Why not you and the girls?"

"It's too much for them." She looks at Marek.

"You go instead," he says. "I'll stay."

She thinks for a moment. "I'm no good driver. No, this is better."

On Saturday morning, Marek and I walk over to the garage where he keeps his car. It's five years old and looks brand new. As we set out, he puts on his driving gloves and holds himself erect behind the wheel, like a man riding to hounds. As soon as we're out of the city, it's as though time has stood still: poplar trees punctuate the horizon, black and white cows graze on flat land, plowed fields spread out behind peeling stucco houses.

We take a side road through Smoszewo and Goworowo and wend our way toward Płońsk, through Sierpc and Toruń, then turn north, following the sharp bend in the river. Marek talks as he drives: about the recent change in the System, about corruption. He speaks mostly English because he wants the practice. "Say you have an aunt" (he pronounces it ount) "that you don't like. She dies, and you inherit all her property. But because you don't like her, you throw away her TV, her radio, her refrigerator, all her things, even though they would be useful to you. You even burn down her house. This is Poland. The ount was Socialism.

"Now Poland is embracing capitalism. The poor are getting poorer. We have learned nothing from other countries. We have learned nothing from the past." It could be my father speaking, the same mix of humor, fatalism, incredulity. People fall on their asses. That's life.

At a small café, I buy us sausage sandwiches and bring them over to an outside table. Baby birds peep in the eaves of a house next door. Marek says, "You did not have children yourself?"

"No."

"Is too bad?" Asking rather than telling.

"I had a career—have a career—that would have been impossible with children. Sometimes I regret it, but it's water over the dam now."

"What is this, over the dam?"

I gesture with my hand, water falling. "It means, too late, you know?"

"I understand. Olesia and I, of course we hope for children who do not have problems. It is difficult, most especially for Olesia. All the time she is at home. If they can go to school, Olesia can work, we can afford a bigger place, but it is not possible. They will not live long time. We will have no grandchildren. We were expecting that Felicia is going to be normal. We are told it is very unusual, two children with the same problem in one family."

"Do you get any help from the government?"

"There are programs. But Olesia says they are bad, she

can teach them better. I tell her maybe sometimes, two days every week it's okay for them to go, but she say no, in the programs, they don't teach the children nothing. Marta would be sitting, that's all, maybe she don't even know any words. I tell Olesia she can be teacher for children like Marta and Felicia, and our children can be in the school. But she says she will have to go back to school to learn to be a teacher."

"She already knows twice as much as most teachers."

"Of course." He shrugs as though things will never change. We finish our sandwiches, watch the birds for a moment, and walk back to the car. Marek puts on his driving gloves, turns the key, and we're off.

I tell Marek that it took my father almost two weeks to reach Bieńkówka after the war ended. No one there knew whether we were dead or alive. He stayed a few days, then hitchhiked to his mother's house in Piaseczno. There, the only remnant of his family was his mother's grave.

"Everywhere, this happens," Marek says. "Every family in Poland."

"Do you remember the war?"

"I was five when it ended. I remember my mother crying."

Driving through the flat landscape, I think of what my father told me about the aftermath of the bombing of Cologne, the dome of the Apostles' Church with its mosaics destroyed, spilled like bright blood over the floor. He'd seen men lying on the ground, limbs blown off, crying for their mothers. A close friend of his was shot in the back by friendly fire. Another friend lost half his face. Mud, bodies stacked into trucks, dead horses.

"People fought all those years," I said, "and then they lost their country anyway. Hitler lied to Stalin. Stalin lied to

Churchill. Churchill lied to Mikołaczyk. Roosevelt lied so he'd get re-elected. He couldn't risk losing the Polish vote in Chicago and New York. So no one knew until later that he and Churchill had already bargained away Poland's borders."

"It's the story of our country." He pronounces it cowntry. "Poland loses an arm here, a leg there. But even when the arms and legs are gone, we don't forget them."

Fifty kilometers further on, the Vistula begins to run shallower and wider. Willows brush the shore. "You see here?" says Marek, pausing at the side of the road. "This is very large farm. Those buildings there—they were houses for serfs in the Middle Ages…Do you know about *szlachta?*"

"The nobles?"

"Yes. They are the ones who elect the king. When the king have to make the important decision, he must talk to them, not like in other countries where the king doesn't have to listen to nobody."

"Do your parents talk about the war?"

"No. They never."

We pass down a long straight road lined with poplars to a T, where, for the first time, there's a signpost to Bieńkówka. 4 km.

Four kilometers! Something wakes in me, so long asleep, I don't know what to call it. I'd crawl those four kilometers if I had to.

The road narrows further. Bieńkówka 2 km.

Two kilometers!

We turn onto a dirt road—I remember it now!—round

a corner, and see the first house in the village. Ludwik and Wira Domański's. The roof has fallen in. And beyond it, my family's house barely stands. The chicken shed is a mound of vines. Across the street, Władysław's house is in ruins. Marek stops the car, glances in my direction, and pats my hand. At a distance, a woman holds us in the blank cup of her stare. I get out of the car and wave, but she moves on without responding.

"She thinks you want something," said Marek, "that you are going to make trouble."

It's too quiet. There are no children. The village looks as though it's frozen. "Where *is* everyone?"

"After the war, they don't come back. They died or maybe went to the cities."

What remains is the river. Clouds push across the sky. A hawk circles above a field. Chickens scratch in the yard of the Belski's house. I turn toward our old house and stumble over a rock.

The roof has caved in. Nettles and lamb's quarters grow wild where the kitchen garden once was. I open the door, and it falls onto my foot. An oak tree stretches up—it looks as though it goes right through the dining room, and upstairs to the room where my mother and father once slept. Someone's taken the woodstove. The water pump and the sink are also missing. Because of the trees inside, the house feels as though it's a river, flowing under the shade of trees.

Marek props the door closed, and we find a path, still in use, leading past the barn and out to the field where my father grew vegetables. The swing is gone. The field is divided in two now, rye newly planted on one side and a cow on the other. I look back at the barn. The stone walls are standing, but the roof has made a bowl where a thicket of weeds and shrubs grow.

I didn't expect all this ruin, although I guess I should have. The only things you can count on are stone and brick. But not those either. Throw a bomb, and they're gone. Mountains and rivers then. But mountains shrink; rivers change course.

I try to imagine leaving my father's ashes here. I picture him in his fields as a young man, sweating, talking to his horses. Suddenly it hardly matters what happens to what's in that box. He's not there. I imagine him swimming in air, free, lying on his back with his hairy chest exposed, his hair slicked back with wind, craggy-faced, forehead swept clean of strife and struggle.

A crow caws in a tree. "I'm going to take the box down by the river," I tell Marek. "You're welcome to come."

"No, no, I remain here."

The box feels more inert than stone. I climb the revetment and look back toward the village. There's no one in sight except a man in a field a long distance away. The wind is blowing shoreward, the river creased here and there by branches and sand bars. Down by the water, I sit on my haunches and look into the middle, where the current is visible, a river inside a river.

Inside the cardboard box is a black plastic box. Inside that is a thick plastic bag, and inside that, the gray, pulverized contents. Not my father. Not his fierce, gaunt eyes, his rackety skin and bones, hair flattened from sleep. Not his cracked voice, his eyebrows shooting in all direction, his old, calloused hands. Reaching in, I bring out a mound of ash and let the wind catch it off my hands. It blows onto the sand and willow bushes, onto my clothes and hair. I lean closer to the water and drop in another handful, which quickens with life when it hits the river. Dry leaves turn in the water, hurry backwards a few steps, and join the main current.

I let handful after handful go.

There's just silence and the lap of water. Near the shore, the water becomes ghosted from ash—white and milky and stretching out further as the current carries it—him. So this is how it ends. The pounding heart, the straining lungs, the arms and hands and legs, the eye-beholder, the ear-miracle, those miles of veins and arteries and capillaries. A swallow dips over the water, grabs an insect and glides forward on an air current. I drop in one last handful and pick up a tiny white shell from the sand and put it in my pocket. As I walk toward the old house, I keep turning to look at the river. It's darker now than it was an hour ago, the sky reflected in it. The clouds are charcoal gray. The sun shines through here and there in pockets of greenish light, a single ray descending from the sky.

Up behind the house in the back field, I open the container once more and pour ashes out onto the grass. A brown cow looks on with vacant eyes and grinds her teeth sideways. I empty the last handful near her feet, retrace my steps and turn. The cow watches me, her ears straight out to the side. She stares and stares and finally bends and eats a mouthful of grass, dusted with my father.

An older man on a tractor drives up the track. The machine coughs and sputters, while the driver's head bobs rhythmically to the beating of the pistons. I look at him a second time. "Piotr?"

He doesn't hear me.

"*Czy to ty, Piotr?!*" I yell. Is that you?

He stops.

"*Co mówisz?*" he asks over the din. What do you say? With a rusted key, he turns off his tractor. It continues to shake and rattle. "*Co mówisz?*" he asks again.

"I wait for the tractor to stop. "Nadia Korczak. Nazywam *się Nadia Korczak!*"

"Oh ho! You can't mean it! Czy *to możliwe?*" Is it possible? He's wearing baggy wool pants, gaping open at the crotch where he's forgotten to button them. His boots are covered with spring mud, the felt ripped at the top. He climbs down off his tractor and hugs me. "What are you doing here?" he asks in Polish.

"Visiting."

"Are you going to stay here?"

"Our house has fallen down."

"The Germans lived in it. It was never fit for anything after that."

"My parents both died, my father just recently. I brought his ashes here."

"Ah, I'm sorry," he says.

"You remember my parents?"

He nods. "Of course. My mother and father are gone too. But you won't believe—our teacher is still alive."

"Pan Wilenski?"

"He taught my children. All three."

"Impossible!…How are your brothers?"

"Michal died last year. *Pompa.*" He taps his heart. "The other lives just there." He points down the road.

"What about Mrs. Mikołajczyk?"

"She died many years ago. None of her family returned after the war."

"None of them, none of her boys?"

"All of them gone."

"And her husband?"

"Her husband was killed in France…After the war, she mostly slept in the barn." He touches a finger to his temple. "At night we could hear her singing to her cows." I can see her holding the accordion in her lap, with its double-sided eagle and rows of buttons. *W murowanej piwnicy,* she sings from a milking stool, as lantern light slides around the stone walls and the cows stare with their vacant eyes.

"I'll ask Teresa to set another plate for supper."

"Teresa Chudzik?"

"Yes, yes, my wife. We are married almost fifty years."

"I can't believe it!"

"Three children we have, two boys and a girl." He gets back on the tractor. "So you come by the house, yes? We'll see you soon?"

"My cousin Marek is with me."

"Him too, of course."

When I find Marek, he brushes my cheek with his fingers. "You know the *Popielec*?" he asks.

"The Day of Ashes?" He takes a red handkerchief from his pocket and wipes at my forehead and chin and slaps at my clothes.

Teresa and I whoop when we see each other. "So tall you are, Nadia! Never would I have known you!"

She's already set out a plate with cold sausages and pickled fish and onions, another plate of bread, another of sliced tomatoes. Piotr pours out vodka. Sitting there with them, it feels that the war never happened, that people never stopped sitting around a wooden table like this, drinking and laughing.

"Emil, remember him?" asks Piotr. "He's working in Bydgoszcz. He has five children, all girls."

"Tell me about your parents."

"My mother died in 1943. My father came back in 1947. He was a prisoner in Siberia. He died only last year. Until then, he lived with us."

"He never had a day's sickness," says Teresa. "After all he went through. One day, he went out to the field and— phoot!"

"He had no use for doctors," says Piotr. "The doctor demands his fees whether he kills the illness or the patient."

"Piotr has no use for them either," says Teresa. "Last year—"

"Never mind," Piotr says. "They don't need to know about all my little troubles."

She looked at him.

"The vodka is excellent," says Marek.

"It's Wyborowa," Piotr says.

"I can't remember when you left," Teresa says.

"In 1942."

"A year after, they hung Gerta Klimas, and Ludwig and Wera Domański," said Piotr.

"The Domańskis? They were the best people who ever lived."

"It was Ludwig they were after. They only killed her because of him."

"Someone later drowned Herr Hahn," says Teresa, "the informer who was living down by the ferry. Piotr and Emil found him washed up on the shore. His hands were bound behind his back. A wire was twisted around his neck. Some said it was Mrs. Mikołajczyk who killed him, but I don't see how she could have gotten him to the river."

"There were reprisals?" Marek asks.

"They took our livestock," says Piotr. "They deported many to Germany. After the war, we had only thirty families left. Half gone. And the ferry no longer runs. Still, we manage to scratch out a life here."

We talk and talk. Before we go, Teresa brings out an old camera with a flashbulb. "*Uśmiech!*" Smile! she says, and the bulb explodes and turns black. Teresa gives me a jar of jam to take home. She floods with tears and says to come back soon.

When at last we're in the car, Marek says, "Okay?"

"Yes, I'm ready."

The sky is deep gray. The only thing visible on the road, behind where Marek has parked the car, is a shrine inside glass, a little statue of Mary and Jesus entwined with flowers. There are words printed on a card, but I can't read them in this light. As the car starts up, a dog barks and runs along beside us until we're almost out to the main road. Neither of us is inclined to talk. Marek's face is lit softly in the panel lights; I'm in darkness.

Once upon a time, I thought of Bieńkówka as a lost Eden, and after the war, a place of sorrow. Either way it's been dream-like and untouchable. What's real? My father once called Poland a nation of victims and mourners. But that's not all of it. There's Piotr's ripped boots and baggy pants, the pictures of their grandchildren, the rye grass coming up in the field, the lace curtains billowing out the window of their dining room, the dog rushing at Marek's car as we drive away. Life hurtling forward, the river flowing, never stopping for anything.

24

We stay overnight with Olesia's cousin and take our time traveling south the next day, stopping to walk by the river, to see the medieval walls of an old town, to just sit and stare at a field. Marek, forever the graceful guide, suggests we take a detour to Zelazowa Wola, Chopin's birthplace, before we head back into Warsaw.

It's close to six by the time the car pulls onto the grounds of Chopin's house. No one else is in sight. Marek wanders into the garden, down a path. I'm left by the quiet house, where Chopin once made his way from room to room. He played softly, with his eyes closed; a waltz wafted into the garden. *Dee da dah. Dee dada, da dah. Dee dada, da dah.* Long ago, there was the wild, urgent longing of a melody. What remains, fading and fading, is ghost sound, the memory of the air vibrating. I stand there a long while, mouth open, listening. A curtain moves in the air. Behind it, the black edge of the piano goes shadowy in the twilight.

My attention is broken by a flock of small brown birds swooping over a half dead tree at the edge of the lawn. A small owl, six inches high, is sitting on a branch. She cocks her tail and flicks it from side to side. The feathers of her body and head are raised. She flies into a tree cavity and hunkers down, her yellow eyes and beak showing. The birds keep harassing her, until the owl rushes out and flies directly at them. At first I think she'll catch one, but it's a gesture. The little birds disperse, and she disappears through a line of poplar trees into the darkening air.

I find Marek leaning over a wooden bridge that spans a pond. The water is covered with vegetation and water lilies; vines choke off trees, and a tangle of shrubbery grows upward toward light. Something disturbs the water, leaving a small circle that disappears.

"They have not cared for the garden," says Marek.

"Perhaps there's no money."

"No money for anything these days. Except new refrigerators."

I smile. "Do you like Chopin, Marek?"

"It's too sad. Even when he's happy, he's sad."

"Maybe he missed this place." I've understood this from being here, the love people have for Poland. There's a kind of gallantry, discernable around the edges, mostly gone now, like ghost music from the last generation, when people died for their country.

We grow quiet. From the vicinity of the house, I hear the remains of the long-gone waltz once more. *Dee dah dah. Dee dada, da dah.*

25

In Warsaw, the air sears the throat like bitter coffee. It's Monday morning, and Marek has gone to his hospital job. The trees toss in a high wind. Olesia will probably stay inside with Marta and the baby. I've called and told her I'm going to Piaseczno to find out what I can about Reba.

The first bus I take goes in the wrong direction. *Ciemnak.* Numbskull. It takes me a while to realize it as we head out of the city. But then something tells me we're going north, not south, and I get off. I'm waiting for the next one to take me back, when an older woman who's sitting on the other end of the bench asks where I'm from.

"*W Nowym Jorku.*"

She waits for me to say more.

"I left here when I was a girl. I'm going back to Piaseczno, where I lived with my grandmother during the war."

"*Jest za późno,*" she says. It's too late.

I think I've misheard and ask her to repeat it.

"*Jest za późno,*" she says, annoyed. "What do you want to go digging around in the past for?" Her hair straggles out from her head like a witch's.

"I'm trying to find someone. My sister."

"What's her name?"

"Reba Altschul."

"There's no one there by that name," she says.

The bus comes over the hill. "This is the right one," she says, as though she's been watching me get on and off wrong buses all morning. She climbs up the steps, takes an empty seat, and gestures for me to sit down next to her. I feel like a child. It seems that our conversation is over. Either I've failed in some way or she's learned all she needs to know. She looks out the window, and I look across the aisle. The bus is mostly empty and feels like the bus of sleep: a man is snoring, and a woman's head nods in front of him. We pass by fields where people are out working, and then a large forest and more fields.

In the late fall, when my mother and I set out for Piaseczno, we traveled in the same direction the bus is traveling now. German families had already displaced the wealthiest Polish families on farms in the northwest and shipped them to Germany to work in factories; it was a matter of time before the same would happen to us. On the road, I slept under a quilt with my mother; in the morning she was up at dawn, feeding the horse, the gray profile of her face hard against the brightening sky. I cried under the cart that held our belongings, and my mother told me to come out and stop my nonsense.

We arrived on my grandmother's doorstep in early November. We knew nothing of the ghettos in Warsaw, in Łódź, in Kraków. We'd heard rumors on the road, but my mother said the stories were too far-fetched to believe: a band of two-hundred fifty gypsies rounded up and killed in the forest, families of Jews gassed in canvas-topped trucks.

The old woman beside me stirs and opens her eyes. "Soon, we'll be there," she says, picking her bags off the floor and moving them to her lap. "Get ready." The bus lets the two of us out at the side of the road along with an older man in a plaid suit jacket. The road into the village is paved now. There are many more houses than I remember. We walk toward the wooden church with its graveyard. "I'm going to stay here a while," I say, pointing to the cemetery.

"I think it will rain," the woman says. She gestures toward a small stucco house across a field. "I live there." She stands in the track, waiting for something.

"*Dziękuje bardzo.*" Thank you. Perhaps one day we'll meet again. She says goodbye and turns and heads across the field.

In the cemetery, the trunk of an old plane tree is bulged and knurled, bark flaking off in patches. My grandmother's grave isn't marked, but my father said she was here, near the only tree in the cemetery. The night we left, she stood with one hand clasped around her fist: *I will endure.* And then her hands held mine tight, so tightly…

It begins to rain.

The rain drips off my forehead and nose as I walk to Babka's house. How many times have I walked here? Now, a new house stands where the woods used to be. The road has been paved. The trees by the side of the road have grown tall.

From the road, my grandmother's house hasn't changed much. Someone has added a room on one side. Faded yellow curtains hang at the windows; parsley is coming up near the front stoop. The outdoor still stands beside the house, where Berndt and the other Germans used to wash. Amazingly, the pile of manure near the barn is in the same place, and the big field has been plowed and recently planted. The silage shed, where Reba was hidden, is gone. *What do you want to go digging around for?* I picture the hole under the floor, the walls seeping with moisture, Reba struggling to her feet.

Many years ago, the national news carried a story. A girl lay in Bellevue Hospital in New York while teams of doctors tried to discover what was wrong with her, why she wouldn't wake. For weeks, she lay in a dead sleep while her mother watched over her. The mystery was solved one night when a nurse discovered the mother injecting her with a drug. The story still haunts me: a mother plunging her daughter into darkness.

There were happy times here too, soon after we came, before Reba. Piaseczno at first felt like a special refuge, almost festive. My grandmother trotted out little pieces on the piano for our amusement, her rough hands stumping over the keys. Later she taught me to play them. She cooked round loaves of bread with the imprint of cabbage leaves on the bottoms. She made a creamed mushroom soup from *prawdziwki*. On special nights, she baked sweet *budyń*, made with potato starch. My grandmother, I think, was a little in awe of my mother because she came from the United States and played the cello. The cello was a holiness.

I know nothing about my grandmother's last days. When we left, there was very little food. The black market had dried up, the forests and fields were picked clean, livestock had been confiscated. We were starving. A light went out of my grandmother. She gave us what food she had, and we had to insist she eat something herself. She had a hacking cough, probably the beginning of the pneumonia that killed her. I don't know how long she lasted, but I do know, from what my father said, that Ewa Jarowska, Stefan's mother, must have brought food to Reba after my grandmother died.

For how long, I have no idea. Perhaps Ewa died during the war as well. My mother had one letter from her, and then nothing.

I knock on the door and wait. No one comes.

I turn away and walk down the road to the house where Stefan lived with his mother, Ewa. An old man answers my knock. I explain that I lived up the road with my grandmother during the war. He says he knows no one named Ewa Jarowska. No, he has no idea who might know her. He closes the door, and I feel like Road Runner kicked out in the street with a large-toed boot. The trail has grown cold before I was ever on it.

I gaze toward the house a while longer, aware that the old man is watching. Around the side of the house, the barn is still standing, where Stefan and I made a nest in the loft after school. And here's the place in the road where he showed me the flapping sole of his boot. There, the tree he and Andrzej climbed when they pelted mud balls down at Rufin Cegielski and his brother.

It begins to rain again, and I walk slowly back toward the main road, past my grandmother's house. There's the plum tree where my grandmother gathered fruit for her thick, dark jam. And the steps where my mother and grandmother sat while the sun slowly set in the summer. There, the tree under which Berndt, the German soldier, used to work on his motorcycle.

One day, I passed him on the road, and the sound of his hammering stopped.

"Where are you going?" he asked.

"To see someone."

"Your boyfriend?"

I didn't answer.

"You're going to see your boyfriend?" I felt his eyes sliding over my face down my neck.

"I don't know."

"Shall I keep you company?" He reached for my elbow.

"No." I pulled my arm free and walked away from him down the road, feeling his eyes dawdle over my back, slow, taking their time, and then the sound again of the hammer against metal.

The tree is bigger now; the place where Berndt stood beside his motorcycle is cluttered with old tires. Across the field, the old woman from the bus lives. I'm almost to the road, when I turn around and head toward her house. I don't know why I'm doing this. I'm part way over a stile when my pants rip on a nail.

The old woman opens the door before I knock, as though she's been waiting for me. "Yes, come in."

The water streams from my hair. My shoes are covered with mud, and I slip them off at the door to the kitchen. There's one small cupboard, painted white, and a table big enough for two. A track is worn away in the linoleum between the stove and sink. A window looks out to the front walk and to the field I've just crossed.

"I told you it would rain," she says. "You're wet."

I wave my hand—it doesn't matter.

"You want a cup of coffee?" She's already up getting it.

"My name is Nadia."

She fills two cups at the stove. "I am Fela. Give me your jacket." She hangs it over the wood stove and hands me an old sweater.

"You've ripped your pants," she says. "Take them off, and I'll mend them."

I step out of them and stand there in my underwear. The

kitchen is smoky and smells of meat. She gives me a blanket and pulls a wicker sewing basket from a shelf. "Where are my glasses?" she mutters. She disappears into the sitting room and comes back with half moons sitting on her nose. I thread the needle for her, and she takes it without a word.

"What are you really doing here?" she asks half curiously, half suspiciously. She gestures to a chair, and I sit down.

"*Próbuję znaleźć Ewę Jaworską.*" I'm trying to find Ewa Jarowska.

"What do you want with her?" she asks in Polish.

"She might know if my half-sister is alive."

"I once knew Ewa. She doesn't live here anymore. She went to live with her sister. I think the sister is in Kraków. Of course she may be dead now."

"Do you know anything more?"

"No."

"The sister's name?"

"No. I don't know it."

While she's mending my pants, she tells me about losing her father and two brothers in the war; her sister was deported to Germany and never returned. She and her mother moved into an abandoned house in Piaseczno, and her mother died a year later. After the war, Fela married a man who left her a few years into the marriage. Their daughter, her only remaining relative, is in Warsaw working for the government.

There's something strange in her, her mind occupied with some vastness. She speaks as though she owes nothing to anyone, is free to live as she wishes, to say what she thinks.

"How did you lose your sister?" she asks.

"She was half Jewish. My mother had to leave her behind with my grandmother. She took me across the border with her."

"She decided to save only one daughter."

"It seems so."

"She suffered because of it."

"I think so."

"I too lost a daughter. But not in the war. My husband turned her against me."

"I'm sorry."

"Perhaps one day before it's too late, she'll come back. You remind me a little of her, you did from the moment I saw you, only you're much taller. If you were my daughter, I'd tell you to forget the past."

"I don't think it should be forgotten."

"What good does it do anyone?" Her laughter is bitter. "Do you see children learning from their parents, parents learning from grandparents?"

"No."

"So you see." Her stitches are tiny. She lays my pants down a moment. "Will you have something to eat?" She gets out a saucer of pickled beets and a loaf of bread and goes back to sewing. "Where is your mother now?"

"She's dead."

She pushes the bread closer. "Take, take!"

I don't know what makes me ask what I do. It's as though I'm in a folded place between two worlds, and Fela lives in the fold, with her white cupboard and stove and linoleum floor and view out the window to an apple tree and rain. "Have you ever forgiven anyone, someone who's done you a big harm?"

She rips a piece of bread in two and puts half in her

mouth. She chews for a moment. "No. Who can you point to when you think of an entire war? At one time, I thought I might one day forgive my husband, but it was impossible. He stole something so precious, it can never be forgiven... And you have never forgiven your *mamusia.*"

"How do you know?"

"I see it in your face. But you *should.* It's different from a husband. She gave you life. You don't have any idea what was in her heart."

"If my mother had listened to her heart, she never would have left here with just the two of us."

"Perhaps one day you'll see her differently."

"The way your daughter will you."

"Don't ask God for the way to heaven. He'll show you the hardest way. For her, I disappeared like a stone in the water."

"I'm sorry."

"Never mind. *Zdrów jak rydz.*" She's telling me she's still healthy. Healthy as a *rydz,* a kind of forest mushroom.

She hands me my pants, better than ever. I thank her and wish her well.

On my way out, she gives me an old umbrella and a jar of applesauce from her tree. I start down the path, turn to wave, and she's there, standing in the rain, watching me pick my way across the field.

The bus is a long time coming. Rain beats on the old woman's umbrella.

Memory is a ditch. A landscape of absence. A distress, a disturbance, the long way home. It's a seaside town that's seen better days. It's a yellow umbrella stuck in the sand in the summer of 1938, the smell of another family's bread and sausage sandwiches. It's my father's woolen bathing suit, navy blue with a white racing stripe down each side. It's the back of his head as he looks out to sea, his cowlick sticking up. It's one single bright sail tugging out toward the horizon, a wide triangle of wind that says, *Forever. The world will always be happy, like this day.*

The sail tacks the other way now. My mother, who's wearing a blue cotton dress striped with pink, spreads a quilt on the sand. By the end of the day, the sand will be everywhere: stuck to my skin, in my hair, between my teeth where the wind has blown it. My father stands in the water, shouting for her to come. My mother strips off her dress and stands in her yellow bathing costume, with a skirt that's a little silly. She turns and runs down to where the water rolls over his feet. I follow. My father's feet are white as fish bones. It's one of the first times I've seen his bare feet; there's something shocking about them. By sunset, they'll have turned bright pink on top.

He's laughing further out in the water now, laughing and telling us to come on. *Come on!* The sailboat has turned again and is heading toward an island. My mother wades in up to her waist; her skirt billows up around her like a yellow jellyfish. She's tucked her hair up with pins, and it's already sliding down her neck. I watch her, curious to see what I'll become when I'm a woman. My mother goes out to my father, further and further out.

She's swimming underwater now, and then my father is swinging me around, whirling me in circles, until only the tops of my toes skim water. We come out to the shore, and suddenly everything stops. An old woman walks up the beach, a woman wearing a woolen bathing costume without adornment, a lump of gray. Her legs are twig-skinny, with indentations where muscles once were. She's brown as bark. I think to myself, *Once she was a girl like me.* It's the first time I've understood the way a life is tucked inside a life, inside another life, all the way back to girl.

On the beach, my mother is sitting next to me on the quilt, my father beside her. I look out to the sailboat once more as it disappears over the horizon. The boat that said, *Forever* is saying, *Farewell.* When I turn to look for the old woman, she's gone.

I'm that woman now, my life nesting inside itself like a Russian doll, dividing and opening, dividing and opening, until there's only a tiny painted thing inside, shaped like a girl-woman, an embryo without arms and legs. In each nesting is my own face, wanting to know what happened, and why.

The bus finally comes. Once it draws close to Martin's place, I get off at a small grocery store for bread and cheese and tomatoes before climbing the ten flights up to the apartment.

I strip and climb into the bathtub, but there's no hot water. I let it run a while, and it's still cold. While waiting for pots of water to heat, I dress again and eat a cheese sandwich on the small veranda overlooking the highway and watch the cars go by. The sun is low in the sky, and the light glows rust-colored through a belt of pollution. I pour hot water into the tub, add cold, and climb in. I feel relieved of some burden, as though the old years have been sloughing off, reconstituting themselves, catching up with the present. There's music coming from somewhere, a few floors down, a sound like a balalaika.

I think of Ichiro. Maybe he's on the street somewhere, maybe bent over a picture frame, maybe with his grand-daughter. I want him to be happy. I've hardly ever known anyone as deserving of happiness as him. He'd scoff at that. He'd shake his head, and his face would go serious. I want to tell him that none of us are the same as the worst thing we've ever done. I don't want Ichiro to live the rest of his life as a penance.

The small puddle in the bottom of the tub is mud-colored. I put on clean clothes, run a brush through my hair, and cut my fingernails. Even when I'm not playing the piano, I feel clumsy when they're too long. The scissors are sharp, curved at the tip. I don't remember buying them—I think they must have belonged to my mother. I switch to the other hand and finish. I'm about to put them away when I catch sight of my hair in the mirror. I feel tired of it, the sheer weight, tired of the labor of washing and drying it, of coiling it around and securing it with pins, of having it slip out from under my hats and having to refasten it.

I lift the scissors and cut off a hunk near my left ear. I could stop here, but I don't. The scissors are small, and I can only cut a little at a time. I look down at the floor, at the long clumps that are falling, and my hands begin to shake. My heart is beating wildly. I reach around and grab a bit over my shoulder and cut.

It sticks out on one side. I look like a hedgehog. I begin on the other side and whack off a big bunch under my right ear. My hair has been my identity, my ballast. I cut more on the right until the two sides match; now there's just the cascade down my back, falling below my waist, mid-thigh. With every cut, I think, *What are you doing?!*

26

Iwake up, lift my hand to my hair, and feel stubby ends.
My head feels light. There's a mad woman in the mirror—as though she's slept in hay, eaten wild turnips. I
open the jar of applesauce the old woman gave me and
eat half—it's tart and lumpy and delicious. Olesia calls and
says that Marta has a summer cold; the baby, she thinks,
may be catching it. I tell her I'll be leaving for Kraków in
the morning.

"It may be a few days before I'm back."

"Piaseczno, it was good?"

"Okay, but no Reba."

Martin's place is mine for the rest of the month, she
says. Their friend will return on the first of July. I don't tell
her about my hair—I still don't believe what I've done. I
tell her I'm planning to check phone books in the library
and come back to the apartment to call possible Rebas and
Stefans and Ewa Jarowskas.

I avoid the mirror after I get off the phone. I find my
hats are all too big now.

My hair moves in the wind—like tiny fingers touching
my head. The bus is full of morning commuters, pasty-
faced, half asleep. I ask a young man with glasses, standing
in the aisle next to me, if he can tell me when we get near

the library. His hair looks a little like mine. Spiky, crumpled from sleep. "*Tak, tak,*" he says.

The library's still closed; pigeons hustle around the sidewalk. I can't keep my hands off my head. It feels electric. A few other people collect on the steps, and the doors open. I ask a librarian for the Warsaw, Kraków and Łódź phone books and look under the *A's* for Reba Altschul in all three. There's one *R. Altschul* in Warsaw and an *R.K. Altschul* in Kraków. Her last name, of course, could be anything now. It seems even more hopeless than it did before I left New York.

In the Łódź directory, there's *Jacob Horowitz.* The Iceman. It gives me a shock. I jot down his address and phone number for Maria, just in case. I check the Kraków directory for Jarowska and find *Aurek Jarowska, Miron Jarowska, H. Jarowska, and Wienczyslaw Jarowska.*

What now? If Ewa's still alive and living in Kraków, she could be listed under her sister's name. What was it? Aunt Beata visited Piaseczno once while we were there, but I can't remember her last name.

I look into space and watch the dust motes drift through the air. I think it's most likely that Stefan would be in Warsaw. I write down possible listings for him, and then it occurs to me that Andrzej Zamachowski would know where Stefan and his mother are. I check the *Z's* in the Warsaw directory and find two *A. Zamachowskis, an A. R.,* an *Armond,* and an *A. Zygmunt.*

Outside the library again, a young man is holding a young woman's hand. "*Powiedziałem, że jest mi przykro!*" he says. I said I was sorry!

"*Nie chcę z Tobą rozmawiać,*" she says. *Okłamałeś mnie.*"

I don't want to talk to you. You lied to me. She pulls her hand away.

"*Nie bądź zła na mnie.*" You're crazy.

"*Jesteś żałosny.*" You're pathetic. She starts down the sidewalk.

"*Basia! Zaczekaj chwilkę...!*" Basia! Wait a minute!

She doesn't look back. He stands on the pavement for a while, and I try to give him space, but he notices me on the steps and says, *Spadaj!* Get lost!

I come out of the library and go around the block to see what's there, and already I'm turned around and don't remember which way is the bus that will take me back to the apartment. I walk around in circles and am about to ask directions when I stumble over a sign for a beauty school.

A narrow flight of wooden stairs goes upward. The steps are cupped with wear, and the banister hangs on by two screws. I climb to the top and find myself in a large room, with two rows of beauty parlor chairs set in front of mirrors. Two young women sit behind a reception desk. One of them is so beautiful. I try not to stare, but I can't help myself. She's tall and willowy and blond and calm, and seems unaware that she's beautiful, which makes her even more beautiful. The other young woman looks at my hair before she looks at my face and asks if she can help me.

"I'd like a trim," I say in Polish.

"Just one moment." She disappears.

The place is full of young women. They're all looking at my hair. A few of them are holding brunette mannequin heads under one arm. There's a great hubbub, but only a couple of other customers: one old woman having a perm, and a younger woman with tin foil all over her head. The receptionist is gone for a long time, and then she reappears from an anteroom with a student. "This is your hairdresser," she says. It's Basia, who just dumped the guy on the street. She looks at my hair, and her hand goes over her mouth, laughter exploding behind it. "*Proszę mi wybaczyć.*" Please. Excuse me, she says.

I tell her I cut it myself and show her how long it used to be. She gasps.

"*Cze mogę się umówić na dziś?*" Can I make an appointment for today?

I seem to fall in the emergency category.

"*Teraz,*" she says, leading me to a chair.

"*Nazywam się Basia.*" My name is Basia. I sit down, and she fingers my hair with her hands and slides a brush through it. She keeps brushing, as though an answer will emerge. She begins to laugh again but regains control. She's asking me something I don't understand. I figure out that she wants to know what kind of cut I'm looking for.

"Not too conservative," I say. "But I don't want it dyed green either."

"*Proszę zaczekać chwilę.*" One moment please. She disappears. I hear conversation in the anteroom, and a teacher with dyed blond hair and large, blue-rimmed glasses appears. She's very serious. They seem to be discussing whether to layer or not.

"I'd like something easy to care for," I say in Polish.

The teacher holds her hands at an angle to my chin. They confer a while longer. Basia nods. "Okay, okay." She looks impatient to get on with it. She's graceful, dressed fashionably, tall with high cheekbones. Long hands, long nails, blocky shoes, mahogany-colored lipstick, a short, spiky hairdo, her hair dyed a deep bronze color.

The supervisor disappears, and Basia gets to work. At

first she's awkward. She can't find the foot pump for the chair. She drops the brush, dips it in solution, and wipes it with a towel. She stops frequently to tell me about her boy-friend—what he said and what she said. She clearly doesn't remember my face from the street. I gather she's just accused him of two-timing her.

"Do you trust him now?" I ask in Polish.

"*Nie.*"

"Then you're done with him."

She looks at me.

"You deserve someone you can trust."

She grows quiet, twists a hunk of hair upwards, fastens it with a clip, and trims the bottom layer under it. "Are you married?"

"Twice, but not now."

"Did either of them cheat on you?" she asks.

"One did."

"So now you have no one?" She twists another hunk of hair and fastens it.

"There *is* someone," I say.

"What will he say about your hair?"

"I don't know."

"I think I'm done with that one," she says. "You're right. I deserve better…You have very nice hair. What did you do with the hair you cut?"

"I put it in a paper bag."

"Can I have it? I won't charge you anything today."

"My hair?"

"To practice. Make extensions."

"Sure, why not?"

She stands in front of me and checks the length of each side. She snips a few stray hairs and begins to dry it. When she's finished, she holds up a mirror for me to see the back. "You notice, I angled it longer to the front. It's the best cut for you. Do you like it?" She looks so young, so hopeful. "It's beautiful. Perfect." We agree that I'll bring her my hair in the morning before I leave for Kraków. She gives me her card, and I head down the narrow stairs, out into the street.

That afternoon, I call the two numbers who might be Reba. A woman answers, obviously wrong, and the other number rings and rings. I get hold of about half the Ewas and Stefans, all of them blind alleys. I go back outside, pick up some groceries, put them away, and start through the list of Zamachowskis. I tell the first man that I once lived in Piaseczno during the war and am looking for Andrzej. I find it very difficult to make myself understood; all my problems with Polish are magnified over the phone. The second possible Andrzej number has been disconnected. *A. K.* hangs up on me. *A. R.* is an Aleksy Radoslaw. I don't call *Armond. A. Zygmunt* puts his wife on because he's hard of hearing. She's also hard of hearing. When she finally understands, she tells me that her husband is eighty-five years old.

I try the other possible Reba again. And then *A.K. Zamachowski* one last time, making myself do it, thinking the person who hung up might have misunderstood, but he hangs up a second time.

I dial the operator and ask whether there are countrywide listings. She doesn't understand at first, but then she says yes.

"How about a new listing for Stefan Jarowska?" There's silence, and at first I think she's gotten annoyed and disconnected me, but she comes on again and tells me no. "How about Ewa Jarowska?" I ask in Polish. Another long silence. And then she says no again. "Can I ask you one more thing?"

The line goes dead.

I call back and ask a second operator whether there's a new listing for Andrzej Zamachowski anywhere in the country. "We do not have listings for the whole country," she says.

"How about Warsaw?"

"I have an A. Zamachowski."

I write down the number, different from any I found in the library. I dial, and the phone rings eight times. I put the receiver down and make myself a sandwich and eat it on the small veranda and watch the cars go by. My mind stops when I think of what I said earlier to Basia: *I have someone.* Is it true, do I want it to be true? I miss him. I add some cash to my long distance contribution sitting on the table and dial New York.

It rings four times, and Ichiro's answering machine kicks in. "I'm calling from Warsaw," I say. "It's about eight o'clock here. It's still light out. I just called to see how you're doing." My voice sounds formal, not how I'm feeling. "I miss you. I'll try again in a day or two. Bye. I hope things are good there."

I put the phone down. I imagine him coming home, pushing the button on the answering machine and hearing my voice. Maybe he'll sit down on the wooden chair by the phone and listen again. Do I miss him because I'm surrounded by strangers, or do I miss him, miss him? I think of the T-shirts he wears when he's working. New Zealand, Khatmandu, Ankarra. When I asked him about them once, he said he goes into secondhand stores and picks out places he'd like to visit. Perhaps he's with another woman. I don't want that to be true.

I pick up the phone one last time, and try the new listing for A. Zamachowski. It rings three times, and a man's voice answers.

"*Proszę*," I say. "*Cze mogę mówić z Andrzejem Zamachowskim?*"

"*Tu mówi Andrzej.*" This is Andrzej speaking.

"*Tu mówi Nadia Korczak.*" My heart's beating like mad. There's a moment of silence on the other end. "Nadia? Nadia Korczak?"

"*W Piaseczno.*"

"Nadia? The little one? Is it true? Where *are* you? I can't believe I'm hearing you!"

I burst into tears. "It's me. I'm here in Warsaw."

"What are you doing? How long are you here?"

"My father died. I brought his ashes to Bieńkówka."

"Ah. I'm sorry… Can I see you? Have you eaten?"

He suggests the Dom Polski restaurant and says it's across the river in the Saska Kępa district.

"Yes, yes, I'll be there." We hang up, and I put on a black top with a low-ish V-neck, and a linen skirt with buttons down one side. As the cab whizzes through back streets, I find a pair of earrings in my purse and a tube of lipstick. I've forgotten a jacket. Some wild, little girl part of me remembers I was going to marry one of them. Andrzej or Stefan. Anything's possible. Stupid! I live in New York.

I'm glad my hair is cut short. I want to laugh out loud. I feel silly-hearted, frightened. There's so much I want to say to him, to ask him. When he was fourteen, Andrzej was large for his age, broad-shouldered, with a smile in his eyes.

He had blond hair that came down to a point on his forehead. His ears stuck out a little, and his face was ruddy and healthy-looking. I remember him sidling up to me and bumping me with a hip. "Hey," he'd say.

One night, Andrzej and Stefan managed to get drunk; they came outside my house and yelled, *Nadia, Nadia! Come out, we want to see you!* I opened my bedroom window, flattered. *Go away!* I told them. And then my grandmother came to the window. It was dark; she didn't know who they were. *Get out of here, you pigs! Leave the child alone!* But I didn't consider myself a child that night.

Looking back on it, I'm surprised I was allowed to be with them at all, or that they chose to be with me. My mother knew Stefan's mother, Ewa, so he must have passed muster. For them, perhaps I was a curiosity, a safe member of the opposite sex. It seemed to amuse them to hear me talk, to wonder about this and that.

There were the secret times with Stefan. And then the times with the two of them. We explored the edge of the woods near our houses, they boosted me into trees, showed me where the wood snails lived; I cried when Stefan shot a bird from a tree.

When my cab pulls up, Andrzej is already standing in front of the restaurant. He's slightly stooped, beefier now. His hair is shot through with gray. We embrace, holding each other tight. "You're *taller* than me." He kisses me on one cheek and then the other. Good humor still pours from him, but that watchful, hidden look has deepened in his eyes. "I can't believe it's you," he says over and over. His hand is tight around my waist. He holds me next to him as though he wants to bump me with a hip. "Nadia! God *damn* it!" He turns toward me all of a sudden and kisses me on the lips. There's really nothing to laugh at, and we laugh anyhow.

The restaurant's located in a villa with a beautiful summer garden. We walk around outside for a few minutes and then go in. Andrzej's shirt is dark blue, open at the neck. We're shown to a table. "I'd have known you anywhere," he says.

"I'd have known you too." He holds my hand tight, on top of the table. I wipe my eyes. He looks across the table and smiles.

"Tell me something," I say.

"I've thought of you so many times, Nadia."

"I'm surprised you remembered me at all. I was only a child."

"But unforgettable."

"How so?"

He orders beer for us both. "You used to stand up to us, you seemed afraid of nothing."

"I *was* afraid. I worshipped the ground you walked on." Saying it makes my eyes fill again. "Do you remember the night when you and Stefan were drunk and came under my window, yelling?"

"No." He laughs.

"My grandmother called you pigs and told you to get lost."

"I loved your grandmother. Do you know, Stefan and I helped dig her grave?"

"I forgot you would have been there. I'm glad it was the two of you...Did you know about Reba?"

"Who's Reba?" He lifts his glass and klinks with mine.

"*Na zdrowie…* You like the beer? It's Żywiec."

"It's good." I have another swallow. "Reba was my mother's daughter by another marriage. My mother hid her during the war. She was half Jewish."

"No, I didn't know anything about her. Stefan and I left for Warsaw after your grandmother died." His eyes curtain over.

"To do what?"

"Hang on, you're hungry, aren't you? Take a look at the menu first."

There's a huge spread: *bigos* stewed with prunes and cognac with a side of *buraczki*, venison, *kotlet schabowy*, *kulebiak*. Andrzej says the fish is usually excellent. I order carp with mushrooms. He orders trout, with a bottle of wine and *zupa szczawiowa* for both of us.

He tells me he's a doctor in a low-income clinic in Warsaw. "Heavily subsidized by the government. I have about 4,000 patients on the books."

"On your own?"

He nods.

"Are you married?"

"I was. We have one daughter, Kassia, who lives in Warsaw and works at the Ministry of Culture and National Heritage. She helps maintain palaces and castles—Kórnik Castle, the Mielżyński palace in Pawlowice…She has a boyfriend. They're thinking of marrying this summer." His hair has been cut, mown really; the cowlick on top stands up straight.

"I have no children, but I'm also divorced," I say.

"When?"

"Twice actually. The last time was four years ago."

"For me, it is five months." He pauses. "There was a

woman at work. Someone informed my wife. It was one time too many."

"But I don't think it's ever one person's fault."

"Why do you say that?"

"I just think it's true."

"It *was* my fault." He seems anxious to prove this point. "My wife couldn't help wanting the sort of life she did."

"She bored you."

"In a word, yes. I did my best…Perhaps I didn't. Are you and your husband still friends?"

"We see each other every so often."

"I never see my wife."

"Do you miss her?"

"I miss the idea of her more than I miss her. That sounds heartless."

"You miss a home."

He nods and has a swallow of beer.

Our soup arrives, and we eat for a few minutes. It's delicious—on the tart side, flecked with sorrel leaves and served over a hard-boiled egg. A waiter pours wine for each of us. Outside, the sky has a bit of light left in it. I feel safe in this place, with its large windows and darkness coming in and globes of hanging lights, surprised at how happy I feel.

"Tell me about Stefan," I say. "Where is he now?"

He stops eating. "He died in the war."

"…Oh, god. He can't have."

"It happened just a few miles from here. Remember we used to talk about going to Warsaw? Had you already left? I don't know whether you knew, Stefan's father was one of the officers killed at Katyn."

"No."

"You know about Katyn, the 4,000 Polish officers murdered by the Soviets?"

"Yes."

"At first the Russians said that the Germans had done it. Stefan grew up overnight when he learned about it, but his mother wouldn't let him join the Underground. Finally she agreed he could work for the Red Cross in Warsaw. We had to lie about our age, but no one cared. If you had two arms and two legs, it was enough.

"We were nurse's assistants in a makeshift hospital in the sub-basement of the old post office. Do you know where I mean?"

"No."

"After dinner, I'll take you there if you want. During the worst of the bombing, we slept there. Of course there were almost no supplies. Morphine when the doctors and nurses could get it, bandages, one operating theater for amputations. You couldn't really call it a hospital. Most of us had no training.

"Once Stefan and I talked about what we'd do if the place was hit. He said he'd run for his life, that it would be pointless to try to save anyone—they were doomed in any case. I said I'd stay.

"In fact, the opposite happened. A piece of the ceiling came down, the whole room collapsed really, and Stefan sustained a head wound. My arm was broken. I put my good hand on his elbow and said, 'Come on, we're getting out of here.' But he said, no, I should go ahead, he'd be along when he could. I left without him. I knew I'd never see him again." His hand resting on the table jerks involuntarily. "Do you know the end of Dante's *Inferno* "...*e quidi uscimmo a riveder le stele?*" And from there we came forth to see again the stars.

"I crawled into the sewer over people with wounds in their bellies, broken legs, a boy whose head was blown off. When I came out, there were the stars. I ran to the river and swam across with one arm. It was September, a cold night. I broke a window and fell into the basement of a paper factory. There were big—what do you call them?—tubes of paper with a hole in the center. By day I hid inside the tube. At night I came out to find food. The end of the war was a few months away. As you see, I survived." He puts down his spoon. "During the worst of it, I said to God, 'If you let me live, I'll give something back.' That's what I've tried to do...But Nadia, I left him there."

"You did the only thing you could have. There was nothing you could have done to save him." I see Stefan standing in the middle of a room without windows, half of it caved in, blood streaming from his head, people in makeshift beds screaming, the world flying to pieces. "You couldn't have saved him if he'd made up his mind to stay."

Andrzej has a large swallow of wine and refills our glasses. "You keep telling me that things aren't my fault." His eyes are shining, and he reaches across the table. "Some things *are* though. And saying it, believing it, is a way of going on. Do you understand what I mean?"

The waiter brings our dinners.

"Beyond what happened to Stefan," Andrzej continues, "two hundred thousand souls died in those two months." His voice turns hoarse with anger. "All that time, the Soviets were across the river. It's the Russians I blame the most. Sitting and watching Warsaw burn, waiting for their opportunity.

"Of course the Germans did things that were so terrible, you could never imagine. They burned people alive in their homes. They herded together women and children and shot them in groups. They threw babies from hospital windows. They starved out the city. But the Russians were our allies, and they betrayed us. That is truly unforgivable. The Allied forces wanted to land in Russia to refuel. They could have brought in supplies. It was only three-hundred kilometers away. And the Russians refused. They didn't lift a finger," Andrzej says. "By the time they granted permission, it was too late, and they knew it. They liberated—this is what they called it—Warsaw in January of 1945, when there was nothing left.

I knew others who died, of course, but no one like Stefan. There will never be anyone like Stefan."

"I'm so sorry. I'm sorry what happened to you...He's beyond being sorry for."

"I returned to Piaseczno to tell his mother, the worst thing I ever had to do in my life." He takes a bite of his trout. "Darling, eat something. You'll be hungry."

We're quiet for a moment. "When was the last time you saw his mother?"

"The day I told her Stefan was gone."

"Do you have any idea where she is now?"

"No idea."

"I thought maybe she'd know something about Reba."

"I wouldn't expect to find Reba. You might not understand how it was here."

"What do you mean?"

"She wouldn't have survived."

We talk about the past fifty years. Fifty years! I hear myself linger over the departures: my mother dragging me from sleep the night we left. Crossing the border from Poland to Slovakia; crossing the Atlantic; two marriages; the death of my mother; the death of my father. Is this how I see my life? I pour myself another glass of wine and drink half of it, look across the table and smile. He has a wonderful face.

"So you are a musician," he says. "I've been to New York once, to a conference on infectious diseases. I was staying—what do you call it?—in Soho."

"Did you like it?"

"It was very extreme, very interesting. But as a people, Americans are like children. They expect everything to turn out fine. Poles, we expect everything to turn out badly."

We finish dinner and the bottle of wine. He squeezes my hand. I haven't heard him laugh yet. I wonder if he ever does.

"Come," he says, "I'll show you where the old post office was."

Outside, we walk to his car and drive toward the center of the city, down a three-lane expressway, the Vistula beside us. And then into a darker part of the city, to a place where an ugly, square fifties-style building stands now. "It was here at this spot," he says. "We were in the sub-basement, as I told you. Somewhere under this Soviet monstrosity—" He means Stefan.

He parks the car. The air is damp and chilly, with a hint of summer in it. "Over here," he says, pointing to a sewer opening, "is where I climbed in." I stare at the opening, how it drops blackly down. I imagine the stench down there, voices echoing off walls, drowning in darkness. The wounded.

We get back in the car and drive to the river. "It's here I swam."

It's nearly dark. No stars. "You're cold," he says, seeing

me shiver.

"A little." He drapes his jacket over my shoulders and holds me around the waist. I look across and can just make out the far shore in the darkness. The water is flowing smoothly with hardly a sound.

"The current carried me. Up there, the river narrows a little."

Andrzej lives on the outskirts of Warsaw in a duplex. Inside, his place is filled with books and wool pillows and wooden folk art. His eyes are soft and bright. I can't imagine what tangle of hurts and grievances would cause someone to leave this man.

"Coffee?" he asks. "Or vodka?"

"Vodka." He goes to the kitchen and returns with two glasses. He bundles me into a blanket, and we sit on a screened-in veranda on a small rattan couch looking out, drinking. The lights of a few cars twinkle.

"Can you imagine coming back to Poland to live?" he asks.

"Could I live here? Perhaps in Warsaw. I feel at home, but my work is in New York. Everything I know is there."

We grow quiet.

Without a word, he turns and takes my head in his hands. He kisses each of my eyes, smoothes my hair, buries his head in my neck. He leads the way to his bed; we hardly have time to get our clothes off. He's awkward at first, as though he's still fourteen, fumbling his way into me, breathing my name, damp in my ear. He's crushing me, and then it no longer matters.

27

Melville once wrote that our souls belong to our bodies, not our bodies to our souls. Andrzej and I loved each other twice more during the night, roaming over each other's faces and skin, lucky to be alive and in each other's arms.

This morning I'm standing on a crowded train bound for Kraków. I feel clear-headed and happy. Earlier, I dropped off my hair for Basia. She was waiting in the huge room at the top of the wooden stairs, the only person there, sitting in a chair with her model head in her lap. "*Zerwałam z nim,*" she said. I've broken up with him.

"*Żałujesz?*" Do you regret it?

"*Nie.*" No. But her face looked disconsolate.

"*Jesteś piękna. Jesteś młoda.*" I told her she was beautiful and young. I had a feeling she'd end up back with him—too young to be sensible.

I'm too old to be sensible. Last night felt foregone, necessary. In fifty years, how much happens: all the losses, all the blunders mixed with fleeting moments of happiness. The work that never ends, never leaves you in peace. The memories; the eleven-year old riding around in me trying to pretend she's fifty-nine. Andrzej and Stefan once befriended that girl. And last night, every time Andrzej moved, every time he smiled, I saw the boy in him. I imagine some needful animal part of me thought I'd mend something in his arms. Maybe he thought the same. Perhaps we did.

Close to morning, Andrzej told me his girlfriend made him promise to stop sleeping with other women.

"Will you tell her what happened?"

"I'll tell her I had dinner with an old friend. I may not even say that much." He wore his self-reproach like an old jacket.

"Is she normally jealous?"

"Yes."

"Do you want to be with her?"

"No."

I raised my eyebrows.

"You make me understand how little she and I have in common. She has a fourteen-year-old son. I don't want to be a parent again. I don't know how to be a parent to a boy."

At dawn, he looked in my eyes. "I hope you don't feel used."

"Why would you say such a thing?" I kissed him on one cheek and the other, and he pulled me in close.

"I want to see you again before you leave."

"When I come back from Kraków."

"I'll wait for you." It's what Stefan once said.

The train is so crowded, the ticket collector is having trouble pushing through the crowd. He's young and perspiring and good-natured. His passengers are like cows in a field: the rain is falling, it grows heavier, we endure. People joke; someone breaks out a bag of peanuts and passes it around. Tarnished, every one of us, small pockets of pride, greed, fear. A mother and child pass through the car on the way to the bathroom. The child is dark-haired, small-boned, his face pale and moon-like, his whole life before him.

28

The train pulls into Kraków. I walk through the station looking for a way out, and a gypsy girl plants herself in front of me and holds up a card asking for money. I give her a little, but she pushes her body close and demands more. I panic and flee out the door with my suitcase, down a ramp that passes under the railroad tracks. I don't understand why I feel so ashamed, except that her poverty is an assault, intense, alive in my nostrils. It's on my skin still, I can touch it with my hand. You feel how much is wrong with the world, how powerless you are in the face of it—like that freezing cold night I was out walking with Ichiro, and we came upon a man in a cardboard box.

On the other side of the tracks is the Opera House; across the street, the Hotel Pollera. It looks as good as anywhere, and I check in for two nights. "Up those stairs," the clerk says, pointing.

The flowered carpet is worn in places, down to wood. At the top, three cleaning women sit in chairs with their hose rolled down around their ankles, smoking and complaining in low voices about the management. They're eating cake with bright pink frosting and look as though they wouldn't get up, not even for the Pope. In my room, a used paper handkerchief is stashed in the corner by the sink; the bed looks as though someone napped in it. Tall windows overlook a concrete courtyard, and Reba comes flying in on the breeze. All at once, anger flaps at my heart like a crow. I don't want to live in this ditch of memory anymore, remembering Reba, always remembering, remembering. If she's alive, I'm going to find her, goddamn it.

Stefan's mother had a comb and brush and mirror, engraved with her initials, given to her by Stefan's father for a wedding present. Once I stood in her bedroom with Stefan, tracing the letters with my fingers. Stefan said he liked his mother's last name better than his father's. At the time, it seemed odd he'd think this. Was it Kryszka he wanted to be? Stefan Kryszka?

I take off my pants and a top with oversized jungle leaves and flowers and put on a more sedate peach-colored dress with a full skirt. I feel dowdy and out of sorts. It's because of my hair. Nothing I used to wear makes sense anymore.

Downstairs, I ask the desk clerk for a phone book, but I can't find Kryszka. *Kryszka, Kryszka,* I mutter out loud. He takes the book from me and lays his finger next to five listings. All the listings are men's names, except for a *B. Kryszka,* on Izaaka Street.

The clerk points me in the direction of the Jewish Quarter of Kazimierz, a part of Kraków that was home to 70,000 Jews before 1939. Only three-hundred people came home to it in 1945.

I walk in the direction of the old town, past a stretch of run-down shops, and finally to a maze of streets that make up the Quarter. The day is windy and the streets silent. I ask directions from an old woman pulling a hand cart. She doesn't understand me and continues on, dragging the cart.

Traveling in a spiral, I find myself on streets pocked with potholes, lined with abandoned buildings, graffiti littering torn fences, with no idea which direction I've come from, or where I'm going. I've seen uglier places, more wasted, but nothing like this. Here, you feel the remnants of a whole people gone, thousands of families, an entire generation missing, like a hole in the world. Their absence tears the heart open: like an ocean liner at the bottom of the sea with all its music and mighty engines, its lights shining, kids running up and down the decks, cooks grilling fish, bottles opening, lovers loving. All lost.

I stumble across Izaaka Street and knock on a door without a number. Across the way, a crew demolishes a building. Metal bites brick. There's a ripping sound, and a wall accordions down on itself. The door opens a small crack, and a stooped woman with faded strawberry-blond hair stands in the opening. She might pass for Ewa's sister, but I'm not sure, it's been so long.

I say my name and ask whether Ewa is there. She seems uncertain and asks me to repeat what I've said. "I'm looking for Ewa Jarowska. I think she's your sister perhaps? Do you know where I might find her?"

"My sister. Yes." She stands out of the way to let me in and leads me down a dark passage to a sitting room. "*Proszę usiąść.*" Please. Please sit down. She gestures to a stiff Victorian horsehair sofa under a picture of some Bedouin-looking men on horseback. I search her face for a resemblance to Ewa or Stefan and think it may be there in her mouth. Something else is there too, beginning to look familiar.

I'm coming to understand that anyone my age or older has a hard story to tell. You can see the war in people's faces: the bombing of Warsaw in 1939, the Ghetto Uprising in

1943, the total destruction of the city a year later. Throughout the country, millions of people were caught between two armies marching toward each other, the Germans in the west and Russians in the east.

"*Herbata?*" she asks. Tea?

"*Proszę.*"

"*Z cytryna?*" With lemon?

"*Proszę. Tak.*"

She disappears. A few minutes later, she brings in a tray and sets it on a little table covered with crocheted lace. She pours out the tea and passes me a plate of cookies.

I explain that I've lost someone in the war, a half-sister. "I believe your sister may have helped her after my grandmother died."

"I had just the one son," she says. "Of course, some people lost many more."

"*Ale ty miałas jego jedynego?*" But he was the only one you had?

"*Tak, jego jedynego.*" Yes, the only one. She passes the plate of cookies.

"*Dziękuję bardzo.*"

"Are you Catholic?" she asks suddenly.

"No."

"Too bad. To go through life without faith."

I wanted to say I have faith, but she goes on.

"Under the Soviets, we lived, yes? But god knows how. We fought the war, but in the end, we were still in prison. Not a single country in the whole world would help us."

"Now you're free of them."

"*Mimo wszystko to nasz kraj,*" she says. Yes, but look at the country they've left us.

"Was your son in the army?"

"In the Kościuszko Squadron. Do you know it? He was trained at Dęblin under Witold Urbanowicz and died in Warsaw in the early days of the war. His comrades told me he was parachuting to safety after his plane was hit. The Germans strafed him on the way down. My mother died the same day."

"Where were you?"

"Also in Warsaw, with her."

"I'm very sorry."

She falls silent.

"I wonder, did your sister ever mention Reba, a Jewish girl in hiding during the war?"

Her eyes fall at the word "Jewish," as though the war were still on. "We did not know any Jews."

"I was hoping Ewa might still be alive. She helped hide my sister."

"I don't know Ewa."

"You don't have a sister named Ewa?"

"I have a sister, Jadwiga. A sister, Paulina. Lila, my sister, is dead. That's all."

"I thought you were Ewa Jarowska's sister."

"*Nie, nie.*"

"I'm in the wrong house."

A laugh comes out of her like dry toast. She reaches her hand over and touches me. "It doesn't matter," she says. "You're a very nice girl."

It turns out she's lived here since the end of the war and worked as a seamstress all her life. Occasionally, she still takes in piece work. Her grandmother on one side was Jewish, but Bogna has kept this to herself. We talk until the middle of the afternoon. She's curious about New York and wants to know what I can see out my window back home, what the buses look like, whether the skyscrapers are lit at night. We trade addresses. As I'm saying goodbye, she gives me a bar of Wedel chocolate. "For your journey."

By the time I get outside, only two walls are standing across the street—naked wallpaper, the bones of a staircase. Windows arch toward sky, a mountain of bricks at their feet. Bogna's building is the last one left on the block, and she seems to be the last one left in it. She told me about the mice; dozens run around at night, over the top of her bedclothes and down the other side.

History books have it that Poland didn't put up a fight in those early weeks of the war. But the Poles had no help and were totally outgunned. Five years later, the Allies helped save Paris, but not Warsaw. Poles were the European underlings, even though the Battle of Britain—one of the turning points of the war—would probably have been lost without the help of Bogna's son's comrades. These same Polish airmen were thrown out of England at the end of the war and made to return to Poland, where a number of them were arrested and sent to Siberia. It makes my blood boil. My father was right. Poland was betrayed at every turn.

As for Ewa. I'm afraid that's it. I've run out of ideas. I'll go to my grave not knowing whether Reba is dead or alive. I want to think there's something redemptive about all that suffering. But I'm a fool to think there might be. It was just suffering—horrible, prolonged, pointless.

There's a synagogue on Szeroka Street. At first I think it's one of the many abandoned synagogues in the Jewish Quarter, but a small sign, high on a gate, welcomes visitors, and I'm drawn through a narrow arched opening into a small courtyard. All the time, I'm saying goodbye to Reba, really goodbye this time.

In front of me, a couple of tourists are putting on yarmulkes. A man gestures me inside.

Uncomfortable wooden seats face a simple altar. The ceiling is water-stained; a cheap red carpet peels up from the floor, while beams of sunlight fall here and there. The light feels pure and strong. I imagine the sounds that have fallen here—a cough, footsteps, human voices praising their creator. These walls have seen more loss than I'll see in ten lifetimes; yet loss isn't what I feel—it's the rags and remnants of human devotion.

Outdoors in the cemetery, two men are working to restore a stone to its footing. Lying everywhere are stones the Nazis kicked over. Slowly, as there's money, the men tell me, the place is being restored. There's a vast hush. A riot of vine and undergrowth grow in the far corners of the enclosure; a canopy of new leaves covers much of the grounds. The cemetery is deserted except for a pair of swallows flitting through the trees.

A wall, pieced together from bits of broken tombstones, stretches up a small incline along one side. Fragments of stone hold images: a pair of hands, a deer, a spiral, a leaf, two flowers, stone tendrils, bound together by Hebrew words.

Back in the main part of the cemetery, a snail moves over the surface of a tombstone. At a distance, an old man pokes around in the greenery, stooping, laying a pebble on a gravestone, pausing, moving on.

That night, I open the hotel windows to the night air, and in comes Reba with the smell of geraniums.

"I'm sorry," I murmur. "You're gone. I don't know how

to find you. Whatever happened, I'm sorry." If I'm honest with myself, I'd hoped to tell my mother across time and space, *See, she was here all along, you could have found her if you'd tried.* But I no longer believe she's alive. Maybe I never believed it. A half moon shines blankly in the sky. Below in the alley, a dark shape moves. Something dislodges the lid of a garbage can, and it clatters onto cement.

29

I feel slack, without purpose today. I could go to the mountains, but I don't feel like being a tourist. I'm *not* a tourist. I've been thinking about going back to Warsaw, but there's nothing for me to do there but buy presents—for Ichiro and Maria, maybe Margot and Peter, if something jumps out at me. I can do that here as easily here as Warsaw. I have five days left. I'm afraid to see much more of Andrzej. My instinct says, See him once more, and call it good. It *is* good. Since our night together, the world feels more generous, as though I've been stuck in the narrow waist of an hourglass and been released…What am I talking about? I'm tired of the sound of my own voice. Honestly. Just shut up, will you?

I want to find Reba.

I pick up my purse and head for the door. On my way out, the concierge downstairs asks in French whether Madame would like to make a reservation for a tour to Auschwitz?

"*Non, merci.*"

I make my way past the Opera House, cross under the tracks to the train station, and buy a ticket to return to Warsaw in two days. Walking down Florianska Street toward the old market square, every doorway is different. Many of them are centuries old, threshold stones worn down by passing feet. Unlike Warsaw, much of the old city remains, full of light.

Just as I get to the open square, the bugler begins playing the *Hejnal* from the north tower of the Kościoł Mariacki, the Basilica of the Virgin Mary. The tune stops abruptly, as it does every hour, in honor of a trumpeter pierced in the throat by a Tatar arrow eight-hundred years ago as he tried to warn the city of approaching barbarians. High in the tower, a shadow passes in front of the stone arch and disappears. An entire city still marks the hour with this story.

Is this what it means to be Polish? This fragment of a song? It's what I tried to say to Ichiro—and what Andrzej said to me: Americans are innocent of brokenness on this scale.

I turn and go into the Cloth Hall, a large medieval building that once was a market center for textiles. Dozens of stalls line the walls, people selling everything from folk art to embroidered linens to teapots. I buy Ichiro a pair of warm slippers. Wrong season, but I hope he'll be glad of them this winter. I think of getting a wooden bowl for Pootsie but settle on an embroidered tablecloth for Maria. I stick it in a bag under my arm along with the slippers and go outdoors. A man is juggling four balls, passing them to a woman. A vendor sells posters. In a narrow wall opening hangs a sign for an Orbis tour. Auschwitz, it says. Without thinking, I buy a ticket.

I never wanted to go. I <u>don't</u> want to go. If I'd found Reba, nothing would have persuaded me to get on this bus. But I feel I owe it to her.

The Polish woman heading the tour has large teeth, badly cared for. One front tooth is gold, the other, grayish. Her hair is cropped short, her glasses are large and red-rimmed, her lipstick reddish brown. Through the mirror, the bus driver's face and brush-cut hair looks sharp as a fox's. He drives fast through the countryside, past newly plowed fields and stucco houses. Beside us, a train with blue and yellow cars moves.

As a child, I loved the sound of trains at night on the other side of the river, the hollow hoot creating a bowl into which the darkness, the crickets, everything living, was poured. Now, I try to think of this train as just a train, nothing more. But what I see are box cars creaking toward their destination, hands reaching out of wooden slats, throats crying for water.

The bus driver pulls into the parking lot at Auschwitz in front of a hot dog stand; the smell of cheap meat fills the air. School children mill about. Some of them look solemn, while others pop gum and horse around. The tour guide lets us off the bus and leads us beside the train tracks, under the gate bearing the three most cynical words ever written—*Arbeit Macht Frei*. Work makes you free.

From there, she takes us across a patch of dirt and down into a concrete bunker. I touch the rough wall and pray that Reba never saw this place. People say that prisoners believed they were being led to the showers. Standing here, I don't believe it for a second. There's no way a person could have come naked into this room without knowing they were going to die. I imagine the doors shutting, the sudden quiet. Above us are trap doors in the ceiling where they inserted the canisters of Zyclon-B. My body's shaking out of control. I want to go back to the bus and scramble into a seat and put my head down on my knees and close my eyes tight.

We pass through a door into a room that looks like an ordinary basement, except for two iron carts on rails, built to hold two bodies at a time. The ribbons of smoke went out this small brick chimney in front of me—here, touch it. We're all crying.

From room to room the tour guide leads us. Everywhere, I say to myself, *This is the worst, it doesn't get worse than this.* There are no words.

Piles of twisted spectacles.

A man's dress coat made from human skin.

A room of human hair, 154,000 pounds of it, dead gray from the gas.

A mountain of crutches, wooden legs, wooden feet, leather corsets with artificial arms attached.

A room of suitcases, labeled with name, number, and year of birth.

A tiny cell where prisoners were packed tight between walls of brick and made to stand until they died.

Photographs of faces. Jews, Poles, gypsies, children. A little boy with ears sticking out.

He would have lived three months at the outside, the tour leader says.

How can she bear this? She looks like a woman who thinks and feels. What must her life be like, coming here day after day?

When we return to the bus, she tells us we're running late. The driver speeds down the road toward Auschwitz-Birkenau.

"Thirty minutes," he says pulling into the parking lot. We walk to one of the few remaining structures. There are concrete toilet trenches, and inside, wooden bunks where four or five women slept hip to hip. Babies born here lived no more than three days. If Reba came here, she'd have smelled the crematorium, she'd have seen the growing mountain of ash. Pray god she died somewhere else. We climb into a guard tower surrounded with dirty windows and look out over bare ground and the few wooden structures not destroyed by the Nazis as they fled.

Back on the bus, I rummage through my bag, tears falling into my purse. I lift out a comb, a wallet, a small notebook, and look at them without seeing. The bus retraces its journey. What does it mean to come from a country where such things happened? To have been alive here then? Outside the window a field borders a forest. I imagine a figure fleeing into the dark trees.

30

I wake to the voice of a bird singing. I'm paralyzed with horror, the ground under my feet cracked open. In a corner of the room that held the seventy-seven tons of human hair, a small dress was displayed in a glass case. A little crocheted dress, white with pink ribbons. It would have fit a baby of six months to a year old. There was a baby in that dress. They took the thread of her breath and snapped it like a twig.

How frantically my mind tries to pass over seventy-seven tons of hair, racing to get away. It says, *Ah, seventy-seven, that's not such a big number. I can count to seventy-seven. And a ton, that's only two-thousand pounds. Anyway, they didn't necessarily kill all those people. Perhaps they just shaved their heads.*

What good did it do to have seen Auschwitz? The horror is so immense, there are no more words to be spoken. If I go home and talk about what I've seen, people wouldn't say it, but they'd think it: I already *know* what happened.

Before yesterday, I knew what happened too, but I don't now. There's something I don't understand. It was in the filthy windows of the guard station overlooking Auschwitz-Birkenau. Looking across that sorrowing landscape, I tried to imagine what had twisted the hearts of those men. I can only think they must have been frightened. Why else would they have thrown away their souls like rubbish?

I think it was Joseph Brodsky who said that fear always has to do with anticipation, with some recognition of the potential for evil-doing, a sense of the worst one is capable of. People are fond of saying the Holocaust could never happen again, but it could, again and again, given enough people who believe in some twisted vision of their own moral superiority.

I get out of bed, unsteady on my feet, and go onto the street. Under the tracks, I buy two bananas and eat them standing up. The day is bright. Shop awnings snap in the wind. I want to talk to Ichiro. Inside the post office, people wait in line to buy a phone card. I stand in line, too, thinking what I'll say to him. *I'm frightened? I'm coming home earlier than I thought?* After half an hour of waiting, I step up to one of the phones. Slipping the card into the slot, I dial his number and listen to the phone ring. There's no answer.

Outside again, near the Opera House, I sit on a bench in the sun with a pastry and bottle of water. A couple walks along the sidewalk. The man holds a leash attached to a big white dog; the woman leads a pot-bellied pig. Its tail wags like the dog's, its pink tummy inches from the cement. The pig snuffles toward me, and I ask the woman if it can have some of my pastry. I hold out a piece, and the pig takes it delicately. I give him another piece and then the dog a piece, and soon, the pastry's gone. I pat the pig on the neck. It feels solid, muscled, and warm with well-being. I get up, and the couple sits down. I feel such fondness for them: man, woman, dog, pig.

Back in the post office, someone yells. *Kiedy?...To nie jest w porządku!* Why? When?...No, it's not all right! Conversations bounce off the walls as the line moves slowly. *Spóźniłem się na pociąg. Co mam zrobić?* I missed my train. What should I do?

Finally, a phone is free. I step up and dial again, and Ichiro's voice comes on.

"You're there! I'm in Kraków, inside the post office, at a pay phone."

"You're all right?" he asks.

"More or less."

"You sound shaky."

"I haven't eaten much." I don't want to tell him about Auschwitz, not right now. "Marek drove me to Bieńkówka. I've also been to Piaseczno, where we lived with my grandmother. I've met some good people, including an old friend. I think I told you about Andrzej and Stefan. Stefan died in the war, but Andrzej lives in Warsaw...The trail's gone cold on Reba." And then I can't hold it. "I went to Auschwitz yesterday." I can't speak for crying. I stand there, holding the receiver, bawling.

"Do you want me to come?" he asks. "You'd need to tell me where Eemo can go."

The phone goes dead. I'm so mad, I feel like kicking the wall. From the dents, it looks as though a few others have had a go. I return to the original line for another phone card, but the grate closes just as the woman in front of me steps up. A sign goes up, "Closed for ten minutes." The man behind me shrugs.

When I reach Ichiro once more, I'm calmer. I tell him I had to wait in two lines. "I'll be okay. I'll be back soon."

"Are you sure?"

"I'm sure."

"It was a hard place for you to be alone."

"Yes."

"You were brave to go."

"I needed to." I can feel myself about to lose it again. "Tell me what's happening there."

"Elsie laid an egg," he says.

"You're kidding."

"I'm saving it for you."

"No, no, eat it."

"She turns out to be a night chicken." He laughs. "There's not much else to report. Eemo's been moaning about Nelson. And there's a pigeon who's been talking to him on the windowsill. It's the damndest thing."

"She found him."

"What?"

"They're in love…"

"Shall I let her in?"

"No, no, you'll never get her out…Tell me about you."

"I took my granddaughter to the playground yesterday, and she fell down and scraped her knee, and I put a dinosaur bandaid on it. My daughter wants to meet you."

"Me too… Yes, I mean." Next to me, a man and woman are having an argument. "I'm sorry, there's a lot of noise."

"I can hear. I miss you. We'll…"

The phone disconnects again, and the card spits onto the floor. A woman next to me bangs her receiver on the wall, shouts into the mouthpiece and stalks away. I can see why people die young here. Judging from the lines, it'll be at least half an hour before I can call back. I mutter goodbye to the wall. He's too far away. I reach into my pocket for a tissue, and instead find the small, white shell of the mollusk I picked up on the shore of the river in Bieńkówka. I hold it in the palm of my hand. I want to go home.

31

The train is due to leave for Warsaw at nine, and I get to the station just after eight, hoping for a seat this trip. Standing in line for coffee is the young black man I met on the airplane.

"Aren't you the guy who's making a film in Warsaw?" I ask. "I met you on the plane."

His face doesn't register anything for a moment, and then it brightens. "What are you doing here?"

"It's kind of complicated." I tell him about Reba. "I was hoping to find an old friend of the family who'd have known something, but I failed. I'm heading back to Warsaw."

"I'm waiting for the camera person to come off the train," he says. "We're doing a documentary on people who were in hiding during the war."

"I'll be damned."

"We got a grant from the Holocaust Memorial Society. We've filmed five people in Warsaw and have three down here. After that, we're heading to Poznan. What's your sister's name?"

"Reba Altschul."

He opens a canvas briefcase, takes out a piece of paper,

and scans a list of names.

"Her last name could be anything now," I say.

"Of course…Here's a Raphaella, is that a form of Reba?"

"No."

He glances at his watch. "Want to sit down a minute?" He puts the briefcase under one arm, pays for coffee, and waits for me to buy a cup. We perch at a table partly occupied by a man in a business suit. "It's a pretty small community," he says. "You want me to ask around?"

My stomach turns over. "You'd do that?"

"Why not? How old would she be? Where was she back then?"

"I'll write it all down…Look, I've just decided. I'm not going back to Warsaw. Where are you staying? I can get in touch with you."

"Meet me tomorrow for breakfast. I'll try to talk to a couple people today. How about the lobby of the Batory Hotel? At seven?"

"I don't even know your name."

"Moses Briggs. The hotel's on Sołtyka."

"*Thank* you, Moses. Thank you." I have both his hands between mine. He looks embarrassed, but I can't stop shaking his hands.

At one in the morning, the garbage can lid in the alley clatters to the ground again. I'm back in the Hotel Pollera and can't get to sleep. I see myself walking down a bombed out street; I tap a woman on the shoulder. *Przepraszam. Excuse me, are you by any chance Reba Altschul?* She looks at me suspiciously. *What do you want?*

I don't believe anything will come of Moses' inquiries. Out the window, the moon looks far away, indifferent.

My mind begins to whir. Ichiro must have heard the way my voice changed when I spoke of Andrzej. Will I tell him what happened? What would I say? I sleep a bit and wake. Groucho Marx's voice pops into my head.

At four, I get up and go to the bathroom. Groucho Marx comes back. He's sitting behind a desk chewing on a cigar, with his caterpillar-moustache and thick eyebrows, eyes looking skyward beneath glasses, a cigar held between two fingers. *If you want to see a comic strip, you should see me in the shower.* Up and down go his eyebrows.

The alarm goes off at six. I get up, take a shower, and put on a pair of khaki pants and a short-sleeved shirt. My hair dries so quickly, it's a miracle. I run a comb through it, put on earrings and lipstick and head toward the hotel. The day is airless and muggy, not a breath stirring. A man with a helmet of black hair sweeps the pavement in front of a shop.

Moses is already there when I arrive. "We can sit in the main restaurant or on the patio," he says.

"How about the patio?"

It's a pleasant spot with skylights and unfinished pine tables and chairs. The buffet table is steaming with sausages and eggs; on one end, pastries are piled high. The tables are about half filled with people. We load our plates, and a waiter comes by with coffee. "Have you noticed," Moses asks, "how Poles eat like South Dakota farmers, but there aren't any fat people?"

"Yeah, how does that work?"

"I don't know." He spreads marmalade on a piece of toast and takes a bite. I know he's found nothing, or he would have told me.

"How did you end up here?" I ask.

"I was in commercial television, and I began having trouble with my heart. The last time I went to the ER, a doctor said, 'You're too young for this.' He was right.

"So I quit. I went out to a monastery in northern New Mexico. It was eight miles from the nearest town. I walked in the canyon and sat in silence for twelve days. When I came back to New York, this documentary job was waiting for me. I don't know what will happen next."

"You've brought some of that quiet with you."

"That's the best thing anyone's said to me all week."

"Is it going well here?"

"The stories are hard…I wanted to tell you, Nadia. I got hold of a few people and asked them about your sister. I'm afraid I don't have very good news. The only small lead was from a woman named Ilia. She has a friend who plays clarinet in a Klezmer band. She remembered him saying that one of the members was in hiding during the war. That's all I know. Not all that promising."

"Do you know the name of the band?"

"You can call Ilia in Warsaw. Here's the number. I'm sorry."

"I really appreciate it."

We talk about his project, which he hopes will make it as a series onto TV. I give him the name of a friend who knows an executive producer in public TV who could possibly be helpful to him.

By one-thirty, I'm on a train heading back to Warsaw, and three hours later, I call Marek and Olesia from the train station to see how they're doing. Olesia sounds stressed out, and I tell her I'll bring over take-out food.

When I arrive, Olesia makes a huge fuss over my hair. "Your beautiful hair!" she says. "Why did you do it?"

"It was time."

"What did you do with it?"

"I gave it to the young woman who fixed the mess I made—she wants to make extensions."

"You shouldn't have done that."

"Why not?"

"People can have power over you when they have your hair."

"Olesia…" I laugh.

"Truly. But turn, let me see…Yes, it looks good. I still liked the long hair, but this is all right."

The baby has a runny nose. Olesia is firing on two cylinders, making an effort. "Did you have trouble with the gypsies in the station?" she asks.

"One young girl called me bad names after I gave her money. She wanted more."

"Ah, you should not have given her anything at all," says Olesia.

Marek looks uncomfortable. "They are a very big problem in our country," he says. "Many of the children don't go to school. Their parents keep them away because they're afraid they'll be harmed."

"They bury their dead standing on their heads," says Olesia, picking up Felicia from her cot.

"That's not true," says Marek. "Who said they bury their dead like that? Here, I'll take her." Olesia passes the baby over. We drink beer and eat Vietnamese spring rolls and shrimp curry. I tell them about meeting Moses and about the woman he spoke with.

"Call her," Marek says. He hands me the phone just as we're about to start on dessert.

"It won't come to anything, Marek. I'll call tomorrow."

"Do it now." Marta is patting my leg with her hands.

I dial the phone, listen to it ring, and hang up.

"Why didn't you leave the message?" says Marek. "Call back and leave the message."

"It's time for dessert."

"Go ahead."

I call back, and Ilia answers. I manage to make myself understood, and she tells me she'll ask her friend when the band is playing next—she thinks they have a regular gig at a coffee house in Warsaw. I give her Marek and Olesia's number and the number at Martin's place.

Marta is in my lap now with her face right up to mine. I kiss her cheeks. "I love you, Marta." She sits awhile, climbs down, and moves to Marek's lap. Ichiro once told me he calls his granddaughter "hotsy-totsy rabbit girl". She convinced him to go down one of those tube slides at the playground. I picture him looking down. He lets go and lands in the dirt at the bottom. Inside the tube is a thudding sound, and he reaches his arms out just in time to catch his granddaughter shooting out.

"Noddy! Noddy!" Marta's patting my leg.

"What, darling?" She's wearing a little short-sleeved yellow top with ruffles, and yellow shorts and sneakers with teddy bears on them. Olesia gets up and gives me the baby to hold while she puts water on for tea. "You're a really big girl now, aren't you?" I say to Marta. She sits on the floor and unties my shoes.

Back at Martin's apartment, there's a message on the answering machine. Ilia couldn't get hold of the clarinetist, she says, but she called a friend who said the group plays regularly at Café Ejlat the second Tuesday of every month. She thinks they might be there tonight, starting somewhere around eight. It's already eight-thirty. The only woman in the group is the singer. I call a cab, grab my purse, and am out the door.

32

The Café Ejlat is so jammed I can hardly get in the door. The band's already playing, a violin, an accordion, and clarinet. At first I don't see the singer. It's an instrumental number, and she's sitting behind the band in a corner, wearing a red top and black pants and low black boots. My heart quickens.

I squeeze my way through the crowd to the bar and order a glass of wine. There's a good sob in the clarinet, and the violinist is excellent.

The group finishes the set, takes a short break, and when they come back, the woman joins them, singing the old song, *Yankele. Sleep, sleep, Yankele, my handsome son, Close your little black eyes.* With the lights on her, she's older than I thought. *Shlof zhe mir shoyn, Yankele mayn sheyner! Di eygelekh di shvartsinke, makh tsu!* Her eyes seem different than Reba's, closer set than I remember. Her sound is gutsy and tender; she sings with her eyes closed and opens them to applause.

The clarinetist announces a song which came, he said, from the composer and lyricist, Mordechai Gebirtig, who died in 1942. It's a wedding song, *Dray Tekheterlekh,* a father giving away his third and last daughter in marriage. He's happy but then realizes he has nothing more to live for. The last line is *Oy, vey, vi pust un bang.* I understand the *Oy, vey.* The rest, I think is probably loosely translated, *This sucks.* As she sings, the singer turns toward the violinist. She looks a little like Reba in half-profile, but I don't feel a jerk of recognition.

They play a few more and finish the set. I go up to the clarinetist, compliment him on his playing, and explain that his friend Ilia has sent me here and why. "I don't think she's the right person, but what's your singer's name, just out of curiosity?"

"Leah. But she's not our regular singer."

"No? What's her name?"

"Reba."

My heart stops. "Reba what?"

"Korczak."

"No way! It's her, I think it's her!" I fling my arms around him, crying, laughing.

"How long has it been?"

"Fifty-one years."

"Whoa…Your sister, you said?"

"Reba! My half-sister, I can't believe it."

There are tears in his eyes. "How did you find us?"

"It's a long story. A guy on the airplane…"

"Gavi—" the violinist calls to him.

"I've got to go."

"Would you mind not saying anything to anyone until I see her?"

"Sure, talk to me afterwards, and I'll tell you how to find her. By the way, you know we're not from Warsaw?"

"No."

"We live in Kraków."

He stands at the mike, and they begin to play again, without the singer this time. Gavi's clarinet wails, caresses.

I go to the bar for another glass of wine. I see my mother leaning against the kitchen sink. I'd give anything to have her beside me now. *Mamusia, I found her.* It would have been the best day of her life.

After the band goes home, I find a pay phone outside the café and dial Andrzej's number. "Did I call too late?"

"No, no."

"I think I've found her."

"Reba?"

"Yes."

"You want to come over?"

I hesitate.

"Don't worry," he says.

"I'll grab a cab."

He meets me at the door with a glass of wine. I kiss him on both cheeks, and we sit out on the small balcony. The night's warm, and the air seems almost clear. "Tell me," he says.

"I don't know for hundred percent sure. But our last names are the same. She must have taken my father's name. If it's not her, it's very eerie."

"What does this mean?"

"Spooky, strange."

"When do you have to go home?"

"Friday."

"You'll go to Kraków tomorrow. Too bad you didn't know before you left."

"It's incredible. If I hadn't bumped into that guy from the plane, if I hadn't met him on the plane in the first place…"

"None of it was accidental."

"You think?"

"Your mother wasn't meant to find her—*you* were, after both your parents were dead." He takes a handkerchief from his pocket and dries my eyes.

"Gavi, the clarinet player, told me she works at a day care center. I'm thinking I don't want to call her on the phone. You think it's bad to just go meet her?"

"It's better. That way, she can recognize you."

"I should have just come and knocked on your door?"

"Yes."

"But I didn't know your address."

"That was a problem." He touches my hair. "You want to go to bed?"

I shake my head.

"I understand. But come sit on the couch. I want to at least touch you."

We go inside and I ask him about his woman friend. "I forget her name."

"Julenka."

"She's Russian?"

"Her father is…but it's over." He takes my hand.

"It's over?"

"I decided to tell her about you, and she called me a bastard and a few other choice things, and it was done."

"I'm sorry."

"We had no future. This way, at least she got to end it."

"*Are* you a bastard?"

"I like *women*. I like *you*." He grins. "It's better to marry than burn. But if you're not married, and if there's no pressure, no dishonesty on either side, what's the harm?"

"No harm. Are we talking about you and me right

now?"

"No. I'm not trying to convince you of anything. I understand about you and me."

"You sound a little guilty."

"I was raised Catholic after all."

"I'd forgotten...Do you still go to church?"

"I go when I feel bad. I went the afternoon Julenka left. She's right, you know. My affections run shallow. It's embarrassing to admit, to you of all people. But you and Stefan were my...what do they call it in New York? Home boys." He touches my hair.

"You're not that shallow, Andrzej. You were married thirty-one years."

"But I was unfaithful all but the first few months."

"Did she know?"

"Some of it. After Stefan died...I told you the factory was abandoned. One wall was bombed before I came there. I was alone for two months, I had no idea how long the war would go on. During the day, Germans moved through the streets, and I had to crouch inside those tubes. After dark, I crept out, knowing I might never get back. I thought, if I drop off the face of the earth, there'll be no one who'll give me a second thought. You were gone, Stefan was gone, my mother and father were dead. In one sense, it freed me. I saw that's the way life is. I could die at any moment. We touch almost nobody while we're here, and we leave nothing behind."

"You think this is it?"

"Yes."

"How do you reconcile that with the church?"

"I don't."

"Maybe I don't have the courage you do—" I make a

circle with my hand and surround his fingers slowly, one by one.

"What about you, when you go back?" he asked.

"What do you mean?"

"What are you going back to?"

"Work. Selling my father's house."

"Do you have a lover?"

"No. But there's maybe someone."

"A maybe someone?"

"Yes." We grow quiet and listen to a dog barking outdoors. "I should go," I say. "You have to work tomorrow."

"I won't sleep yet. Nadia," he says, suddenly serious. "When will I see you?"

"Will you come to New York?"

"If I have the money. When will you come back?"

"Someday. I don't know."

"I don't want you to leave."

My stomach turns over. "You have my address." I kiss him. It's starting all over again, and I pull away and put my fingers on his lips; I pick up his hand and kiss his palm. "I'm going to go now." I stand up, pick up my jacket and hat and start for the door. "You'll be all right?" I ask, turning.

He comes over and smoothes my hair. We remember at the same time, I have no car. "Wait a minute, I'll drive you home," he says.

"Don't worry. Just call me a cab."

"No. One moment." He goes to the bathroom and comes back out into the hall. We stand together outside the door while he uses three keys to lock up. "You know about the Polish Mafia, don't you? You must be careful at night."

"Yes, I know." But I don't really know.

We're quiet together, everything said except what's most obvious: *You feel so dear to me.*

He drives slowly. The streets are quiet. It feels as though we're gliding somewhere out of this world, to another planet. He pulls in front of the building where I'm staying and buries his head in my arms. We both cry. I watch the lights of his car fade and disappear as he drives down the block.

Inside the borrowed apartment, I sit on a low chair. Andrzej never recovered from the war. It's made him guarded, sad, lightly attached to the world. And guilty. Damn it, he couldn't have done anything if Stefan had thought it best to stay. I hope he understands that, but it hardly matters now. The past is unredeemable. Stefan is past praying for. The young, hopeful thing once alive in Andrzej is gone.

I put on my jacket, find the keys, and go outdoors. Not far away, Marek is asleep next to Olesia; Marta and the baby are close by, so close their parents can hear them turn in their sleep. I'm not frightened of the Polish Mafia. The street feels still and kind tonight, this night when I found my sister.

I walk one block over and head toward the Vistula. An older man comes toward me on my side of the street. As his life passes, I feel a tug like gravity. His footsteps recede. Maybe he feels something similar, wonders briefly who I am, what I'm doing. The river's before me now, more beautiful at night, its industrial color hidden by darkness. The lights of a bridge shine in the water and shimmer into four circles of light. It's impossible to think of Andrzej swimming this expanse with one arm—all of it is impossible, what's been lived, these tiny capsules called bodies—his body, my body, these bits of heaven mixed with earth.

The air has stilled and warmed. Across the river, hanging at the horizon, is a brown belt of polluted air, softened at its underbelly to a light ocher. The sky is lit underneath where the moon is rising, and beside the brightest patch is a single star. *To see again the stars.* Or perhaps it's a satellite let loose in the firmament, a vessel shuddering along the hard pull of earth, this hope and home, all there is.

33

I know her the moment I see her. It's mid-afternoon. I'm standing outside a chain-link fence near a street on the outskirts of Kazimierz. The day care center is housed in a three-story brick building. The fence surrounds the outer perimeter of building and land. Inside, about fifty feet away from where my hands are holding onto the wire mesh, is a concrete playground with a slide and sandbox, a few swings and a large open area. The yard is full of teachers and children. Reba is pushing a boy on a swing. She's facing me; the swing and the child hide her momentarily and fall away, hide her and fall away. It's like a slow strobe, as though I keep finding her and losing her. I notice every flicker of her face, the way she holds her arms at her sides and then lifts them for the push. At one point, she runs under the swing, and the boy—a small child with dark hair and pinched face— laughs. After a few more pushes, she says something to him, and he shakes his head. I think she must have asked whether he was ready to get down. She goes back to pushing him.

Her body has thickened, not unattractively. She looks ample, solidly rooted, and moves easily, although there's a slight limp when she walks back behind the boy after running under the swing. Her hair is almost entirely gray and twisted back at the nape of her neck, similar to the way I used to wear mine. Her eyebrows are dark and her mouth full, her eyes soft and heavy-lidded. She's wearing loose-fitting pants and a T-shirt.

A fight breaks out between two girls near her. Reba leaves the swing and puts her arm around both of them. She talks to one and then the other. The one who's crying tells her something and the other child yells something that sounds like, *To nie moja wina!* It's not my fault! Soon after, they wander off in opposite directions. Reba looks up and sees me standing by the fence. I wave, embarrassed, and she turns away.

I flee down the street. I don't know how to introduce myself. I have no brain, only happiness.

On my way back to the day care center, there's a flower stand. I buy a bunch of yellow daisies, and the flower man folds them into a cone of white paper. The rain falls all at once, drenchingly, and by the time I get to the front steps, parents are arriving to pick up their children. One by one they go in and come out with a child. Some of them look at me suspiciously. The sun has come out, and rain is evaporating from my blouse and pants and hair. It occurs to me that teachers may use a different door. I walk around the building; on one side, a door leads to a narrow parking lot where a few cars sit. What to do? If I stay around the side, she could walk out the front. If I stay in front, she'll jump in her car and drive away. I park myself closer to the side door where I can see part of the front walk.

Three teachers come out, two from the side door and one from the front. It's after five now, and the procession of parents thins out. A small boy runs out the front door and falls partway down the steps. His mother drags him up by the arm. I begin to worry. Maybe I've missed her. Could she have left early? Another teacher leaves from the side door, and then no one comes or goes for five or ten minutes. I could go inside, but it doesn't feel right. I decide I'll introduce myself to the next teacher and ask her when the center closes.

The side door opens, and Reba comes out.

I'm paralyzed, stuck to the pavement. I watch her make her way down the walk to a small beige car, open the door, get in, and start the engine. She backs a few feet, turns the wheel. I'm running now, through a barrier of low shrubs and into the driveway. She's moving forward, and I wave my arms. She locks the driver's side door, checks the rear view mirror, and stops. I smile and hold out the flowers, and she rolls down the window. I touch my throat to tell her I'm unable to speak.

"Reba?" I say finally. "Reba Korczak?"

"I thought you were a crazy woman," she says later, laughing. "I remembered seeing you earlier in the day." She stops the car behind a bunch of parked cars, leans over and kisses me, and starts up. We're headed for a grocery store. She wants to give me dinner but has no food in the house.

"What would you have eaten?" I ask.

"*Ziemniaki*," she says. Potatoes.

"You can give me potatoes."

"*Nie, nie.*"

"Or I'll take you out to dinner."

"I want to feed you."

She drives slowly, a little erratically. We have this in common: tears close to the surface. At the shop, she picks up cheese, crackers, green beans, oranges, beer, fish. "You will stay with me tonight of course," she says, pushing the cart toward the cash register. "When do you need to go back home?"

"I've checked into the Pollera Hotel. My flight leaves Friday night from Warsaw." I have a concert two days after I return.

"Too bad, too bad. You have to go so soon. I'll drive you to the hotel and pick up your things. Tomorrow, I'll call in sick…This is my sister!" she says to the check-out clerk. "Fifty years! Today is the first time we've seen each other in fifty years!" She kisses me on the hair. I can't take my eyes off her. There's my mother; there's Reba again. I could die of happiness.

Her apartment is in the southern part of the city in an older neighborhood, on the fourth floor of a building with maybe thirty other apartments. Inside her place a low barricade doubles as a counter and eating space, separating the living room from an efficiency kitchen. Off to one side, a small patio overlooks the street, and to the other side is a bedroom with just enough space for a double bed. In the living room, a white cotton rug on the floor alternates squares of black and gray; the couch and chair are upholstered bright blue and sit on shiny metal legs.

She cooks without fuss and stops every now and then to look at my face. "You looked like Mama then."

"I was thinking *you* did." And then she grabs up my hands. The yellow daisies are in a green vase on the patio, sitting on a small table where she sets two beers and two plates. The light is just leaving the sky; the evening feels fresh from the rain. She's cut up fresh dill and sprinkled it on the fish. The green beans have a cheese sauce. I keep looking at her face in wonder—*moja mamusia, moja siostra.*

Over dinner, Reba wants to know the route my mother and I took after we left. She asks about Nebraska, what people do there. I try to describe how big the sky is. I tell her about New York in the fifties when I was first there, about my first walk-up on Christopher Street, the radio bawling out of the floor below, the Horn and Hardart on 57th Street, the women who dispensed the nickels lickety split, the macaroni and cheese served in brown oval dishes, the coffee that poured from a dolphin-head spout.

"You would have loved it."

She asks about the night clubs, about who played. And about Jimmy and Peter. "Did you love them?…Do you miss sex?"

I laugh. "Sometimes. Do you?"

"Yes."

"Would you ever want to live out of Poland?"

"I think of it every now and then. I like the Netherlands. I lived in Prague for a year after I left my first husband. I thought of staying there," she says. "I don't know why I came back. I was thinking of becoming a translator and going to Japan or maybe the U.S., but I never looked into it. I thought I'd miss the children."

"Your English is very good."

"I thought some day I'd come to the U.S. and try to find you…Look," she says, holding up her hand next to mine.

"What?"

"The same."

It's true. Big wide hands. She pulls me to my feet and drags me in front of a mirror. I have a gap between my two front teeth and she has only the suggestion of one, but we both have wide, full mouths. Wide shoulders. Wide-set eyes. "The same smile," she says. "Same mouth. Same eyes. The biggest difference is the hair and the height."

"I just cut it. It was down to here."

"Wah! What did you cut it for?"

"I was tired of it. I didn't know I was going to do it."

"Do you remember this?" she asks. She turns and opens a squeaky bureau drawer and brings out Aunt Dot's yellow umbrella. It's faded almost to white. The silk is so rotten, it rips in several places when she opens it.

"I can't believe you still have it." It makes me cry.

"How did you get so tall?" She wipes away my tears with her sleeve.

"I grew six inches the year I left here."

"Did you eat beef?"

I laugh. "Morning, noon, and night. You'd have grown tall too. I was hungry for years—I ate like a horse."

She looks in the mirror again and stands on tiptoes. "What would it be like?"

"Am I the only family you have left?"

"Yes. Of course."

We drive to the Hotel Pollera, and Reba comes in with me. "I'll talk to him," she says as we approach the desk.

She explains who I am and says it's impossible for me to stay at the hotel, we have only these two nights together. She ends by saying of course I can't pay for the night. The night clerk gives in with hardly a fight, opens the till, and refunds my money. I leave some of it as a tip, run upstairs and come down with my suitcase.

Back at her place, Reba opens two more beers, and we sit on the patio. The light's faded completely from the sky;

her face is illumined from the lights inside the apartment. She uses her large hands as she talks, the way my mother did. "How long have you been looking for me?" she asks.

"My father told me about you only a few months ago."

"And for me, I didn't know where you'd gone. I thought most likely the U.S. Do you remember the field behind the shed?" she asks in Polish.

"Of course."

"Mama would take me there at night. There was a path into the woods, and we'd go there. I didn't know you were leaving until a few days before you left. Mama told me your grandmother would look after me. After you went away, I was angry. I felt like shouting. I almost wanted them to find me. Every night I'd go outside, I didn't care if there was a moon or not. Sometimes I'd sit on the edge of the field in plain view.

"Your grandmother became sick a few weeks after you left. She wasn't strong enough to overcome it. One night, she looked so bad, she was shivering. She said if anything should happen to her, Ewa Jarowska—you know her, yes?— Ewa would help me. Your grandmother came once more when she could hardly walk, and that was the last I saw her. She used to read the Bible and pray with me. I missed her very much.

"There were three days and nights when no one came. Finally Ewa found me and told me your grandmother was dead.

"And then her son was killed. One night, she came and told me she was going to leave Piaseczno to be with her sister and she'd find someone to look after me. The next night, she said she wasn't going to go after all. She was going to move me during the next dark cycle of the moon to an outbuilding closer to her house.

"But one of the Germans living in your grandmother's house discovered me. He waited for Ewa to leave, took me to the barn, and did what he wanted with me. The next night, he told Ewa he'd kill us both if she kept coming. She came once more, but I told her to stay away. From that point on, I saw no one but him. He moved me into the barn, into one of the horse stalls.

"He saved me once when an officer found me, but in return I was his slave. Berndt was his name."

"I remember him," I murmured.

"He fed me. He brought buckets of water for me to wash myself. Once, he brought me a piece of chocolate. And once, he brought a knife. He sawed off my hair with it. He said I'd given him lice. I hated him. I'd hear the sound of them coming home from wherever they went in the day; I'd hear them washing at beside the house, and I knew he'd come. He told me if I tried to escape, he'd find me and send me on a transport. He told me what would happen at the other end."

I reach over in the dark and hold her hand.

"I thought of trying to kill him, but I had no strength. I didn't want to live anymore. I found a piece of rope. I tied it to the beam, but the rope was rotten. I sawed my wrists with a shovel. When he saw what I'd done, he left me alone for a few days. It's surprising, Nadia, what one gets used to.

"At the end of the war, I knew things were happening because of how he behaved. He talked about his life back in Germany, about his fiancée. He looked scared; he began to beat me. There were more planes overhead. And then he stopped coming. This had happened before, and at first I thought he'd be back. I crept out one night toward the house. I could hardly stand. The street was deserted. The house was completely quiet. I made my way toward Ewa's house and knocked on the door. She told me the war was over."

"Do you know what happened to him?"

"Someone said he was killed. They said there was a dead German in your grandmother's house, but I don't know if it was him…I lived with Ewa for some time after that. We had a few vegetables in the garden and two laying chickens. She said I needed to change my name—it was still unsafe for Jews—which is why I am now Korczak."

She looks across at me in the darkness. I can just see her eyes.

"There wasn't enough food. So in 1946, I moved to Warsaw with two other women, to a house with one wall missing. There were two children belonging to the women, and three orphan children. Rich people who came back to the city wanted their silver polished. They buried it before the war, or it was in the fires. That's how the three of us earned money for food. It kept us alive…After a time, I began to take care of orphan children at the centers. I still know many of them."

"Do you have children of your own?"

"No. I was married in 1950 for two years. I had to leave him. He'd been captured by the Russians in the war and spent three years in Kolyma camp. He kept food under the bed in secret. He was young, but he was a broken, violent, crazy old man. I thought I could help him.

"In 1962, I met Lucjan. We moved to Kraków, but he was killed in an accident. Three years ago. A piece of machinery fell on him and crushed him. They brought his body here, up the steps. He was a good man." She looks suddenly tired.

"I'm so sorry."

"We had many good years. He's still here. I talk to him…" She gets up and turns on a light inside, close to the patio. I hear the toilet flush. The refrigerator door opens and shuts. Reba hands me another beer and then puts her hands on either side of my face. "I can't believe it!"

I squeeze her hand and make beads of kisses from her hand to her elbow. She laughs. "Do you miss *mamusia?*" she asks.

"Sometimes I do. But we weren't very close."

"Why is that?"

"Maybe I never forgave her for taking me away from here."

I stopped. "She could have stayed."

"That's not true," Reba says, looking at me closely. "Don't tell me you don't know why she left."

"What are you talking about?"

"She found the German, Berndt, in your room in the middle of the night, half undressed."

"You knew this?"

She nodded.

Suddenly it all made sense. One night at my grand-mother's house, my mother woke me and made me get out of bed. She told me she was cold and needed me to sleep with her. Until we reached the U.S., I was never allowed to sleep alone.

"Did your father know?"

"I don't know."

"She tried to get me identity papers. She paid a lot of money for them, but when they were delivered, they were crude, impossible to use. We'd have all ended up dead."

"I can't believe she never said anything," I said quietly.

I think of a particularly cold winter: my mother walking on ice, crossing the river from Bieńkówka to the market on the other side, the light through the bare trees lacy and low. She grew smaller as she crossed. She was young then, already torn between two daughters. Her life was haunted, you could see it in her eyes, hear it when she gasped for breath, all the secrets filling her lungs until it used up the air, like a house burning, the windows and doors sealed shut.

Nadia, Nadia, how ignorant, you are! I could have spent a lifetime loving her. The eyes of the lofty shall be humbled. I'm so ashamed. I think of the dreams she wrote down. *I don't want to die.* But she did die, the day she crossed the border with only one of us.

34

Reba falls asleep beside me in the double bed and wakes suddenly a few minutes later. "You found me…" Her words are slurred with sleep. She smiles. I touch my head to hers in gratefulness and listen to her breathe.

I think back to my mother's dreams, written in pencil. In so many, she's lost something. Or she's done something she regrets. Or she's left something behind and is frantically searching. All at once, I see her as a woman, a flawed being, separate from me, worthy of love. I wish she were here in this bed with the two of us. I wish I had five minutes with her, just five minutes! to tell her I was wrong, that she deserved more than I gave her.

Perhaps that's her gift to me—that I'm hopelessly flawed too, and worthy of affection. Not in spite of those flaws but because of them. Who doesn't suffer?

Sadness suddenly overwhelms me. I get up quietly and go into the living room. I can picture my mother running across a field. When she gets to the other side, she turns around and runs back. Her life revolved around impossible choices: between her cello and her first husband, between Reba and my father, between Reba and me. I walk out onto the porch and down the steps. I'm only wearing a T-shirt and jeans. My feet are bare. Somewhere in one of the buildings, a baby cries. Instinctively, I put my hands over my ears. I've never been able to bear the sound of a crying baby, even at this distance, muffled through walls and glass and cement.

I always thought I never wanted children. But all at once, I know the truth. My throat gives way to great choking sobs. I'm astonished. I sit on the ground under a tree, my feet stretched out in front of me. The baby stops crying, but I go on, thinking of what's been lost, thinking of my mother. She'll end her sojourn on earth in the faces of her two daughters, divided by an ocean.

In the morning, Reba brings me a cup of coffee in her nightgown, her hair down her back, and climbs back into bed. She tells me that she dreamt she heard two cows singing in a barn.

"They were you and me," I say, laughing. I feel as though I hardly know her. I don't know what she'll say or do. We sit and lean against the wall.

"Did you get up last night?"

"I went outdoors for a while."

"You were okay?"

"I'm sad about Lili."

She grabs my hand and kisses it. "Don't," she says. "Do you know this? *The one that doesn't know and thinks she knows is a fool. The one that doesn't know and knows she doesn't know is a child. The one who knows and knows that she knows is wise.* It's no one's fault. It's life. So…" She puts her finger on my lips. "I'm a fool too." She laughs. "And *mamusia* was a fool for being quiet."

"She did her best."

"It's true."

"She missed you terribly."

"Do you think so?"

"My father said she thought of you often."

"It helps knowing this."

We get dressed, and she makes more coffee and toast with marmalade. "Today," she says, "I'm thinking we can go for a drive."

"Whatever you want, I'm happy."

"I'll take you to the Wolski Forest. There's a zoo inside it. And the forest is very beautiful."

"I'd like that."

"And we'll stop and have a lunch somewhere." Soon, we're in the car, traveling west from Kraków. The day is overcast and mild. "…You know, you smell like her," Reba says.

I laugh.

"It's true. There was a hole in the trap door, do you remember? When I put my nose up to it, I could smell who was standing above. It was hard to tell you and *mamusia* apart. When that German found me, I smelled him before he opened the door." She turns off the main road.

"It's unbearable to think of you down there."

"Anyway, it's finished. Do you know I used to sing songs to make the time pass?"

"I never heard you."

"In my head. I made up many songs. Some of them, I still sing…I must pay attention, I always miss the next turn. There'll be a small, brown sign. Help me look—I think in another two or three kilometers."

"My father liked small roads like this."

"Was he kind, your father?"

"Underneath, yes."

"My father liked to tell me I was like my mother," she says. "*Kurwa,* he called her." Whore. She paused. "But Mama was lonely. I don't blame her."

"I doubt you've ever blamed her for anything," I say.

"Maybe if I grew up with her, I would—but when she was gone, I made her perfect in my brain. The only thing not perfect was not to see her." A hare runs out in front of the car, and she brakes suddenly and misses it.

"Is that it?" I ask. We've just passed a small road, marked with a sign. She stops, backs up and turns down it.

The sun comes out. Still driving, Reba shrugs out of an overshirt, down to a rust-colored T-shirt with a V neck. I think how beautiful she is. She has her hair down today, pulled back in a barrette. For the first time I notice the scar on her wrist.

She pulls into the parking lot, and we buy tickets and enter the zoo gates. Pygmy hippopotamuses wallow in a jungly hollow filled with water; a herd of Przewalski horses graze at a distance. We spend a long time with the gorillas. At first, we share the fence with a school group; the kids make faces, jump up and down, bang on the plexiglass, and then they leave. The gorillas move over the ground and through the trees like water, trailing long arms. Two family groups are spread over a tree-strewn enclosure. A male gorilla holds a baby. One of the older females, with a wrinkled face and tired eyes, lies on the ground, turns over on her back near the fence, and looks at us over one shoulder.

"I feel bad for them," I say. It's odd, and probably not an accident, that Reba and I have ended up here, surrounded by animals locked up. It's the way I've thought of her all my life, the only way I've ever seen her, until yesterday. Impossible, then, to imagine this place, this sunlit day, her arm around me.

"Are you hungry?" she asks.

"Yes."

We stop at the zoo café and order soup. There's so much I don't know. I don't even know if she minds my asking questions, but she doesn't seem to. She tells me she had four siblings in her family, all boys. "My stepmother had a nervous disorder. My father beat her when he was drinking and sometimes when he wasn't. He also beat the boys (all but Srulek) —and me when he could get his hands on me. That probably saved me, you know? When they began to empty out the village, I ran. Most children wouldn't have. It was in the middle of the night. If I'd been more loyal toward my family, I would have shared their fate. Srulek was the youngest. I was very protective of him, and I grabbed him without thinking.

"Do you know he never said one word after we left? I told him he must be quiet, that we would die if he made noise. And after that he never spoke again. Not even a whisper."

"I never knew him at all. Only his face."

"He used to play games on his fingers in the dark. Taps on my wrist followed by a certain number of fingers. He'd worked out a kind of—you know the Chinese boards for counting?"

"Abacus?"

"Yes. He had a system with taps and fingers for multiplying and dividing."

"He couldn't have been old enough."

"He was five. And you should have seen him draw

before the war. Dragons and mythical beasts, bridges and boats…If he'd lived, I suppose he'd have had no end of trouble with this world." Her face grew sad.

"Did you ever return to your village?"

"Once I went back. Maybe five years or so after the war. But there was nothing to return to. I learned that my father was killed on the night I ran away. Also my oldest brother. The rest were put on a transport. Only three people from my village returned after the war."

We finish lunch and walk down a deserted path. "I would never come here alone," she says.

"I think of you as having the courage of five."

"It's what people say to anyone who's had misfortune." There's a touch of bitterness in her voice. "'Oh, you're so brave,' they say. Who says it's bravery? During the war, I just wanted to stay alive. I had no more courage than anyone else.

"The worst times were after Srulek was gone. I thought I'd go mad. I begged *mamusia* to hide me inside the house, under a bed, in a wardrobe, anywhere I could hear the sound of voices. I wasn't like Srulek. I don't have the kind of… what do you call it? Inside life. I'm not well suited to being alone."

"Now too?"

"I don't like the sound of my own footsteps on the floor. It makes the hair on the back of my neck stand up, you know?"

"I have a parrot who keeps me company."

"A bird in your house?"

"Named Eemo. You'll meet him when you come. He's full of himself, never without something to say."

A solitary man walks toward us, pale and sulky-looking.

Reba grips my hand. He passes, and she whispers, "I don't trust that one."

"Do you want to go back?"

"Didn't you feel something strange about him?"

"No."

"Something sneaky?"

"No."

"Is it just me?…Do you know the movie, *The Thirty-Nine Steps?* Where the girl is followed by two spies and she tries to convince the hero that her story is true, but he doesn't believe it, until he finds her in the morning with a knife in her back?"

"You think I don't believe you."

"You believe me, but you don't feel the danger."

"We'll go back."

"No. It's all right." She takes my hand and leads me to a lookout. From here, we see the Cloth Hall, the Kościoł Mariacki, and the spires of many old churches in Kraków.

"Are you okay?"

"I drank too much last night," she says.

"Me too. Does your head hurt?"

"Not so bad."

She passes me a bottle of water. We sit on a log in the shade while the clouds pass over. A chipmunk comes out of hiding and runs around. On the nights when the moon was young, Reba and my mother went into the woods and sat on a log. I imagine stars and the sheltering boughs of trees and small rustling things they couldn't see. I feel drowsy and close my eyes. I'm trying to remember what Reba said. *The one that knows, knows she doesn't know. The one that doesn't know and knows she doesn't know…*

After a time, she stands up, the log shifts, and I slide

onto the ground. She laughs.

"Do you know about teeter totters?" I ask. I feel cheerful in a manic, overboard way, ready to cry, shout, I don't know what.

"What is teeter totter?"

I look around, drag the log over to a flat rock in the clearing. "Help me lift it...Now you sit on that end and I sit on this end."

I push off and she goes down. She pushes off hard, and I come down with a bump. She bumps upward as I bump down, and then I push off hard again. *Bump!* Her face takes on a ferocious look. *Bump!...Bump!* We get wilder and wilder until the log rolls off the rock, and we're both lying on the ground, laughing. We pull the log back on the rock and have another go. *Bump!...Bump!* Our eyes lock on each other, our legs spring up and down. Suddenly, the log breaks while she's up, and she crashes to the ground. I rush over, and she's laughing helplessly. I brush her off, and she stands and brushes me off, whacking my bottom hard for good measure.

Walking back, I say, "I've never heard you sing."

She goes a little way up the path, turns back toward me, closes her eyes, and begins a song that has no words. It sounds as though she's grabbing the tune out of the air, but I swear, I've heard it before. Is it from our mother? Dreamed by one of us? Something Reba composed in that darkness? Her voice is naturally low, cello-like, with a big resonance. When she finishes and opens her eyes, she looks surprised for a moment, as though she didn't expect to see me.

"I'm humbled by you," I say.

"What does that mean?"

"You sing so beautifully, my heart stops."

We start back along the path, my arm in hers, our stride matched. I feel like the luckiest person alive and tell her so.

"But you hardly know me," she says.

"It doesn't matter. I know enough to know how lucky I am."

Around a corner, the pale, sulky man is coming toward us again. "Quick!" she whispers, grabbing my hand and reversing direction.

"He's harmless, sweetheart," I say in English.

"He's not!"

I look over my shoulder as he walks off the path between some trees. She's trembling, and her limp seems exaggerated. I take her arm and make her walk past the place where he's disappeared, back toward the car.

"What did you do to yourself?" I touch her knee.

"It's nothing." She doesn't say anything more. I want to snatch this fear from her, lift it from her shoulders.

"Come back with me to New York," I say.

"I have no vacation. But at Christmas. Maybe at Christmas."

"I can send you a ticket. My father left me some money."

"Yes? Truly?"

Over dinner, she comes back to the man in the woods. "I made too much of it."

"You have reason enough, god knows."

"Sometimes I behave stupidly."

"Stupid is the last thing you are."

"I'm not so sure."

When she's falling asleep that night beside me, she says, part awake, part asleep, "I'm afraid I'll disappoint you,

Nadi."

I kiss her hair and rub her shoulder. "Why would you think that?"

"I'm not anything special."

"I saw you with those children, how they loved you." I take her in my arms. "And do you imagine that anyone in the world sings as beautifully as you do?"

"If I come to New York, maybe I'll embarrass you with your friends, you know?" She begins to cry.

"There's no one who won't love you the way I do." I dry her cheeks with my fingers.

"What about the man you spoke of? Maybe him."

"Shhh." I put my fingers over her lips. "You're speaking nonsense. Turn over, and I'll rub your back." It takes a long time before her shoulders relax.

The next morning, she drives me to an early train. What I carry back to Warsaw is her hair flying upward, her laughter, a faded yellow umbrella shot with holes, her terror on the path, the sound of her singing, like something born in the woods.

35

I've just come from saying goodbye to Marek and Olesia and the two girls. I feel sad at the thought of the ocean that's about to separate me from them, from Reba, from Andrzej. Before I left, Marta kissed me on my palm, a big, wet kiss, and then on my lips.

Already, half of me is in New York. I feel myself speeding up, getting ready. I hate the expense, the effort of living there. I hate it when it's cold and rainy and the wind blows through the tunnels of streets. But there's hardly anything else I don't love. I love the way someone will smile at you on the subway when you don't expect it. I like how, when you go to a big show at the Metropolitan, people are willing to wait in line for hours and stand ten deep to see a drawing by Leonardo. Or the way Zabar's mobs up on a Saturday afternoon and you can hardly move, and a voice comes over the loudspeaker telling you that the white sturgeon caviar from Italy is on special. Or the chance meetings with strangers. The day before I came here, I met someone from Warsaw. I heard her accent waiting in line in a store and asked her where she was from. She's an artist living in Brooklyn Heights who works at a restaurant in my neighborhood. We're meeting after I get back.

My seat turns out to be two-thirds of the way down the plane, next to an aristocratic-looking Polish woman with a sun-worn face. She looks to be in her late seventies, early eighties, and speaks nearly flawless English. She tells me she's Lidia from Toruń.

"I had a teacher in Piaseczno during the war," I tell her, "from Toruń. She was a great admirer of Copernicus." I haven't thought of Pani Lewandowska in years. Before the war, she taught history and literature at the university. She spoke Polish, Russian, French, German, English, and Serbo-Croatian. We went to her house for classes and sat in the kitchen with the curtains drawn. Because the Nazis had abolished school for non-Germans, she could have been shot if they'd found her teaching us. Every day, she wore a brown short-sleeved dress with a pin-on yellow crepe rose. Her undershirt straps fell down her arms, and she'd push them back to her shoulders, and a few minutes later they'd be looping over the tops of her arms again. I never understood how brave she was until later. "I live near Copernicus' house," Lidia says. "He changed the world with his *De Hypothesibus Motuum Coelestium a se Constitutis Commentariolus*. Not only did he know the Earth wasn't the center of the universe, but the universe…" She paused while the plane raced down the runway and lifted off, "…the universe was much bigger than anyone thought. It was the greatest revolution of human thought the world had ever known. If the Earth was no longer the center of all creation, then humans—" She cackles a little. "We got put in our place.

"You know?" she says. "I have to be reminded every day that I'm not the center of the universe. But you know what will finally do it?"

"What?"

She lowers her voice. "Disintegration. My knees are bad. And I'm nearly bald. That's why I wear this ridiculous hat." It's a small skull cap, maroon. Wisps of hair poke out around the edges.

"There are many ways to be put in your place," I say.

She looks interested. "How so?"

"I grew up thinking I was a beloved only child. It turns out I have a half-sister in Poland. All my life, I believed unflattering things about my mother that have turned out to be untrue."

"So what are you going to do now?"

"What do you mean?"

"How are you going to live?"

"I don't know."

"I'll tell you what you must do. You must endeavor to go from an upper case Me to a lower case me."

"Are you talking about me or you?"

She cackles. "Me, of course. I never stop talking of Me." She looks out the window, down to the ocean. "During the war, I worked in the Underground. I lost many comrades. I've written seven books of history." Her voice trails off for a moment. "But none of that matters as much as what I'm about to do. In a few hours, I'll meet my granddaughter for the first time." She rummages in her purse and brings out a picture of a young girl who looks half African, half European. She's wearing ankle socks and little black pumps. A small white dog is licking her face. I take the picture in my hand. The shadow of a grownup person falls onto the grass, over the little girl's arms and legs.

Our meals come. Lidia looks at hers suspiciously and eats a small bit of salad. She puts down her fork. "Do you know this?" In a cracked voice, she sings the *allemande* from a Bach French Suite.

"Yes, I do."

"In Bach's music, you hear suffering. But you also feel that he set out in his sun-chariot every morning to create a new day."

I smile. "I like that. When I get home, I'll play that piece and think of you."

"You play?" It's as though she's seen me for the first time.

"Yes."

"Do you love anyone?" she asks suddenly.

"Why do you ask?"

"Because I regret certain things. Once I knew a Norwegian man who capsized in a fishing boat in the North Sea with three other men. He was the last to leave the boat. When it went down, it sucked him under, but he came back to the surface. He was in the water for five hours. His tongue was frozen, he'd lost the feeling in his limbs, he was close to death. When a helicopter spotted the men, they tried to lift Ura into the helicopter first, but he dived back into the water. The other men had families, he told them, and he had none. I could have had children by him, and I said no. Do you see what I'm saying? There's more to life than cleverness."

"What happened to him?"

"He died." She closes her eyes.

I think of a time in Nebraska, standing and watching several engines pulling a long line of freight cars across the prairie. In the distance, the train was silhouetted against the horizon, car after car moving against the sky. Life passes like a train, like clouds, never still. The thin chest of the old woman slowly rises and falls next to me. *Do you love anyone?*

I never answered her. What have I been doing with my life?

We switch seats just outside New York because Lidia likes to be on the aisle when a plane is landing. I lean my forehead against the plane's window. It's a clear night, millions of lights. The horizon spreads darkly to the east, an indistinct line where water meets sky. The plane is buffeted by wind. The captain announces that the gusts are unusually strong, that we'll be landing from the south. The landing gear whirs and crunches as it comes down. The bottom falls out as a gust hits; there's another sudden lurch, and I'm flung against Lidia. I glance at her hands as they fist at the bottom of her blouse. I reach for one of them and squeeze. It's icy cold.

"It's okay," I whisper. But maybe it's not. The wind pushes us sideways, and the flight attendants lurch toward seats and buckle themselves in. It would be too stupid if life were to end now. The plane drops again, and someone in the back cries out.

Lidia's lips are white. She whimpers a little. "Do you want some air?" I ask. She nods, and I adjust the nozzle toward her face. I see her as I imagine few people have ever seen her. I unscrew my water bottle and pass it to her, but she shakes her head. The bottom keeps falling out of the sky; the cabin is too quiet. A violent gust throws us to one side, and I take Lidia's hand and hold it.

I picture the façade of 217 West 102nd street, hear my key in the front door, my footsteps on the stairs. The plane does another bounce, and we're under the clouds, within sight of the ground. The announcement for landing comes on. I rub Lidia's hands a little, trying to bring life back into them, and a few moments later, the plane bangs down.

There's weak applause all around us.

Lidia adjusts her hat and turns to me. "Thank you." She fishes in her purse and brings out an ivory-colored card. *Lidia Buda-Wielkopolski, ul. Kataszyna 23/25, Torun, Poland.* "I hope we shall meet again," she says, already beginning to return to herself.

As she stirs, I smell cigarettes and am reminded of my father. He never smoked before 1939, but by the time he got out of the army, he was going through two packs a day. After a time, he cut down, but he kept it up for forty years. My mother smoked through half of those years. I began in my twenties and quit in my fifties. I always liked the way a cigarette let me think. I liked smoking with my father, the way the smoke wove between us. *I'll see you in the air.*

I miss him with a jolt of pain.

At last, we shuffle off the plane. People spill into customs with bags and bundles and baby carriages; the Polish language disappears into eddies in the crowd, swallowed up by English, French, Swahili, Russian, more tongues than I can count.

The customs officials move people through fast, and Lidia Buda-Wielkopolski passes through the double doors in front of me. A small child runs toward her, and Lidia staggers and half picks her up. But the child's mother grabs the little girl away, and says, "What's wrong with you? That's not Nana." It's sad and funny all at once, and then the real daughter and granddaughter push through the crowd, and I watch them meet, Lidia's old face pasted against a young cheek.

"Nadia!" At first, I think it must be another Nadia, but I turn, and there's Ichiro's face.

"What are you *doing* here?"

He circles my waist with his arm and grabs a bag hanging from my shoulder. "You look wonderful. Let's get you out of here."

I stand there stupidly. "I can't believe you've come."

"Of course I've come."

I kiss him on the cheek and the other cheek and hug him tight, and then we stand in front of the empty, rumbling conveyor belt in a crowd of people.

"You cut your hair," he says. "I like it."

"I didn't mean to. I mean I didn't know I would…"

"It suits you."

"You got a haircut too."

"Last night with clippers." I brush my hand over his hair. It's soft and makes me want to cry. Everything makes me want to cry.

The first bag appears, and people crowd nearer. Lidia is holding the little girl across the way. Her daughter is next to her, skinny as her mother.

"I found her," I tell him.

"Who? Reba?"

"Yes."

"You've seen her?"

"I came from there yesterday."

"My God! What does she look like?"

"A little like my mother. Like herself. You should hear her sing! She's going to come here—there's so much I want to tell you." A shadow passes over. What will I say about Andrzej? "There's my suitcase!"

Ichiro edges through the crowd, picks it off the conveyor belt, and we head for a cab.

My mind's blurred with double vision. *A green votive candle flickers in front of a war memorial. Two horses stand in the darkness as Marek pulls onto the main road from Bieńkówka.*

I hardly remember the ride to West 102nd. Ichiro's black shirt is open at the neck. A van rolls along beside the cab, pulling forward, dropping back. Ichiro tells me that Elsie's laid a second egg.

He carries my suitcase up the stairs, sets it inside, and we go next door to his place. In the other room, Eemo doesn't hear me at first. "And then...and then," he says, rummaging through his brain, trying to straighten out the narrative line. "Mr. Rogers, haha. Haha...Goddamn it." He goes nuts when he sees me. "Oh weyy! Hello, Eemo, hello hello! Mr. Rogers haha! Hiho Silver!" He beats his head up and down. "Bird-o, friend-o!"

"Look at you! You handsome boy!...He's looking good," I tell Ichiro.

"We did okay. But you must be exhausted." He picks up Eemo's cage for me, and we look in at Elsie. She's shaking a piece of limp lettuce as though it's a worm. Her feathers, sheared off on the street, have grown back. She's plump, with a little upturn at her tail. The short feathers of her neck gleam mahogany in the light. She pecks at the leaf, shakes her head, pecks again.

"I'm beginning to get the hang of what she's saying," he says, setting Eemo's cage down. "I read an article the other day that said some birds are as smart as chimpanzees. I don't think chickens are quite up there. But this no-good parrot—huh, Eemo. You don't like Elsie, do you."

He carries Eemo next door for me and sets him down by the window. I ask if he'd like something to drink. He says no, he'll leave me to get settled. He hugs me and kisses me on the cheek and closes the door behind him. He's gone too quickly.

Eemo is suddenly quiet. He cocks his head and eyes me through the bars. "Mr. Rogers, haha?"

I open the cage door, and he jumps onto my shoulder, lifting his foot and scratching the side of his head while I light a candle on a small table. "Way down upon the Swanny River! Far far away! Far far away! Way down upon the Swanny…!" His eyes are bright. He rubs the top of his head on my hair, as though he's saying, *What did you do with it?*

I slide open a window and put on a CD. The orchestra shimmers for a moment and the violin begins its gorgeous rising line. It's Perlman playing Prokofiev, playing so beautifully you can hardly believe your ears. I listen to the music and stroke Eemo's head. The air from the open window warms my skin. It's close to midnight. I put Eemo to sleep under his night curtain, pour myself a drink, and open the window as wide as it'll go. The rays from a brightly lit building shine upward into cloud. Below, someone's parking a car. The tires squeak against the curb; a woman gets out, grasps her dress on both sides of her hips and gives a tug.

I want to know where the spirit goes: the house that collapses, the breath that stops, the old tree that falls to the ground. I want to know if those things are contained in what's straining at my heart to get out.

All at once I notice something on top of the piano—a sculpture, a little bigger than the palm of my hand. A woman with flowing skirts is riding an old-fashioned bicycle, its big wheel made from the lid of a can, the small wheels, from gears. Her face and torso are out of blue clay; her mouth is open in an O, as though she's singing. A green parrot sits on her shoulder. Standing there, I find the question that's been forming ever since I got off the plane and heard him call my name: how long, how long have I waited for you? I think of the picture Ichiro once showed me, himself as a boy, his hair freshly brushed, his brother leaning against him.

I find his slippers in the suitcase and stand in the middle of the floor. I want his arms around me, and mine around him. I want to tell him he was with me in Poland every day—on the shore of the river that Andrzej swam; standing beside me before that little girl's crocheted dress; listening to the trumpeter in the north tower of the Kościoł Mariacki. And then I'm in the hall between our two apartments, all the vanished days gathered there. From inside, there's a faint tapping. Marta's wide, flat face comes to me, her hands like leaves. *Go on,* she says. *Knock.*

ACKNOWLEDGEMENTS

My gratitude to my mother, Margaret Brooks Morse, who bicycled through England and Germany in the summer of 1938 during Hitler's rise to power; and to my father, Philip Weber Morse, who served on a submarine tender during World War II in the waters of the Pacific. I owe you my life and the sensibilities that gave rise to this book.

A special thanks to Jane Gelfman, Sena Jeter Naslund, and John Wetterau who read the manuscript and offered expert suggestions and insights at a time when they were most needed. A thousand thanks to Alisa Wolf for her invaluable reading and proofreading.

To Ula Kowalczyk, Irek Ginda, Stanisław and Anna Zielinski, and Bogusław Dobrosielski, for your kindness in Poland.

To Tamiko Onodera, Phoebe Reynolds, Toby Mostel and Aileen Winter for help with information on Japanese culture, the restoration of picture frames, and the life of parrots.

To Pawel Lech for translation assistance, to Yale J. Reisner at the Ronald S. Lauder Foundation in Warsaw, and to Sarah Zarrow, Ruth Gruber and Dariusz Zgutka.

To the Allen and d'Entremont families for providing writing getaways on North Haven island and Pubnico, Nova Scotia; to Akiko Masuda, and to Marya and Miguel Schwabe on the Big Island.

A number of books were helpful for adding to my understanding of Polish culture and history, in particular: Alan Adelson and Robert Lapides, *Lódz Ghetto* (1989); *Janet Flanner's World, Uncollected Writings* (1979); Gerda Haas, *These I Do Remember* (1982); Eva Hoffman, *Lost in Translation* (1989); Czeslaw Milosz, *Selected Poems* (1980); Lynne Olson and Stanley Cloud, *A Question of Honor: The Kosciuszko: Forgotten Heroes of World War II* (2003); Art Spiegelman, *Maus*.

To Susan Williams, Louisa Packness, David Moltz, Barbara Potter, Nicole d'Entremont, Patty Ryan, Jonathan Gaines, Elizabeth Young, and Lobsang Toldan, your support has meant more than I can say.

I'm immensely grateful to Kate Kennedy for reading this manuscript patiently and sympathetically from its earliest incarnation to its completion, and to family members, Catherine Seager, Alan and Georgia Seager, Finn Wetterau, Shannon Koller, Edith Allison, and Alan Morse. And to John Wetterau, thank you for lighting up the days so bright in every direction.

Made in the USA
Las Vegas, NV
23 August 2021